Ulysses Exposed

N GRAY

Ulysses Exposed is a work of fiction. Names, characters, places and incidents are the product of the author's imagination or are used fictitiously. Any resemblance to actual persons, living or dead, events, or locales is entirely coincidental.

Print ISBN 978-1-990998-29-4
First Edition July 2019
Second Edition December 2021
Edited by Novel Approach
Published in South Africa by Cutman Press
Cover by Deranged Doctor Design

For Mom, miss you.

One

The air was cool, the sun warm against my face. I was sure it was evening in Sterling Meadow, and not daytime at the beach.

I pushed my fingers into the sand, but the hard concrete beneath shattered my dream. My eyes fluttered open. I was lying on cold ground, looking up at the dark night and the shiny stars scattered beautifully like diamonds across the sky. There were no clouds to ruin my view. It was peaceful and serene.

I glanced to my left, but an ache exploded at the back of my head, my blood trying to thump its way out. My eyes flitted to the sky once again. My pulse thundered in my ears, my eyes clouded over with dark swirls and stars of my own, forcing me to lay still for a breath.

When I lifted my left arm, I couldn't raise it any higher than my body before pain caught me in my ribs. I made a small yelping sound and lowered my arm back to the cold ground.

I raised my right arm, lifting it all the way to my head, and felt something wet and sticky in my hair. Bringing my hand into view but there was no bright red; only the dark maroon liquid dripping from my fingertips.

I didn't remember much before I saw the stars in the night sky. I didn't remember how I got here, wherever here was.

With effort, I sat up, leaning on my right elbow, but my vision swirled and a headache blossomed. When I could focus again, I scanned my shadowy surroundings. A large dumpster was in front of me, full of garbage. Now that I could see it, I could also smell it. The stench wafted upon the air; the disposal trucks hadn't collected in a while.

Behind the dumpster was a brick wall with boxes on the floor and trash strewn around. It looked like an average alley, except it's not a place that anyone should lay in.

I tried to sit, my breathing now labored, but pain tore through my abdomen and flooded all the way to my toes. A soft cry escaped my mouth. Beads of sweat trickled down my face as I pushed with both arms until I was leaning against the wall. In a half-sitting, half-lying position, I slowly bent my knees and noticed that my jeans were ripped, a wound on my left thigh visibly oozing a dark, murky liquid.

It looked like claw marks. The only animal large enough to inflict a serious injury like this was a were-animal.

Were-animals had been living among humans for a while now; along with all the other monsters, vampires, witches, warlocks, fairies and dragons, to name just a few. We, the humans, tried not to be food for any of them, and there were laws protecting us against the monsters.

Being attacked by any were-animal, if it didn't kill me, could leave me infected with the viral strain or virus of that specific were-animal.

Shit!

If I survived—which was a big *'if'*—I would turn furry once a month when the moon was full. I didn't want *that* to happen. Nobody did.

I wiped sweat from my forehead and pulled the rest of my shirt out from the waistband of my jeans, looking to see why there was so much pain in my side. I wore a black vest beneath a black blouse, and the two pieces of clothing came out of my jeans easily as I pulled. Pain cut through my side again and I clenched my jaw. I lifted the two shirts higher, exposing my black bra, but as I was the only one there, there was no embarrassment necessary.

I froze when I saw an empty shoulder holster, a gun nowhere in sight. I hoped I had a license for the gun—humans got jail time for carrying a weapon without that piece of paper.

With both shirts pulled high, I saw the wound. There were small chunks of flesh missing from my left-hand side; the soft delicate meat between my hip bone and ribs was gone, chewed and swallowed by something with big teeth. The wound had tears splitting from it that almost reached my belly button, like the were-animal had wanted to rip me apart.

As I pressed gently on the wound, blood gushed thick and heavy from beneath my fingers, and the night sky swirled before me again.

When I came to a few seconds later, the wound was still trickling blood. If an organ had been nicked by the animal's teeth, there might not be enough time. If I was going to survive, I needed to do something quick.

I unbuttoned my blouse and steadily slipped it off my shoulders. With my teeth and hands, I tore the blouse in half, scrunched one half into a tight ball, and pressed it gently against the wound on my side. Tears began to trickle down my cheeks and onto my chest. I pulled the vest down to cover the wound and to hold the make-shift gauze in place. With the other half of the blouse, I flattened it out and twisted it so that it looked like a long rope and tied it around my thigh. It was the best I could do to stop the bleeding without having a belt.

With the tourniquet in place, a sharp, shooting pain vibrated up my spine and down to my toes as I secured the knot on my thigh, allowing me the freedom to hold the wound on my side closed with both hands.

I felt all the pain; the tearing of the bite wound and the pulling of the clawed wound as the adrenaline tapered off. I lay quietly, concentrating on my breathing and contemplating my next move.

I could scream for help and try to crawl out from the alley. But, there was a problem with that. I didn't think I would be able to move with this hole in my side, and I didn't know the neighborhood. There could be monsters leering around every corner, hungry to taste fresh human meat, and the moment they saw me they'd pounce. Vampires loved blood. Were-animals loved flesh. Witches could use me for their spells.

Shit.

My pulse hammered in my ears, and tiny sparks fluttered in my vision. I needed help. Now!

I sat straighter against the wall, my body positioned slightly to the right so that the wound on my left wasn't compromised. As I bent forward, something thicker than tears ran down my face. I'd been so concerned about the wounds on my leg and abdomen that I'd forgotten about the wound on my head. I wiped it away with the back of my hand to find more of the dark, thick liquid. This had to be the worst evening ever.

My breath caught in my throat when the sounds of men talking and footsteps nearing. They were almost at the opening of the alley. There was maybe three or four of them. I didn't know if they were good men and would help, or whether they would finish the job the were-animal had started. If they were vampires and saw all this blood, then I was the perfect victim. I hadn't heard of a vampire that could resist so much blood. And no were-animal could resist biting into fresh flesh. I was a *Happy Meal* to go.

But, I needed help urgently. I had to risk being discovered or I'd die a very slow, and painful death.

At first, I cried out softly. When they didn't respond, I cried out louder. The talking stopped, and the footsteps slowed down. I glanced over my right shoulder to see the entrance of the alley and rested my head; it was too much effort to keep my head up. In the light, I saw three of them, one slightly ahead of the others. They were staring at me.

Their eyes glowed like a cat's would when in the dark. The men were were-animals, and I was potentially vulnerable prey. The man in front, his face concealed in darkness, stood painfully still; possibly tempted at the dying woman on the ground.

I cried out again, this time a whimper, as the pain ripped through my body.

The men spoke quietly to each other, then the man in front nodded.

I closed my eyes for a second and when I opened them again, two men entered the alley and headed toward me. When they reached me, one crouched down and showed me his hands, letting me know he had no weapons and meant no harm. I hoped.

I tried to speak, but no sound came out. I cleared my throat and tried again. "Help me," I whispered.

"Your leg is bleeding. I will try to stop it and then pick you up. If we don't help you now, you will die here." He looked up at his friend and then back at me. "Can you hear me?"

"Yes." I nodded and swallowed hard. I think everyone around the block heard me swallow. "Please help me."

"Give me your belt," the man said to his friend, lifting his hand to wait for the belt. When he had it in his hands, he wrapped it around my left thigh and fastened tightly to stop the bleeding. When he pulled on it, to fasten the belt into place, I cried out until the night swallowed me.

Two

I woke in a stranger's arms. He carried me like a sleeping child with my right arm draped loosely around his neck. I tensed and grabbed hold of his neck as if I would fall.

He must have felt me move because he patted me gently on my arm.

"It's okay. I've got you. I won't let you fall," he said, gazing down at me. "I'm Sebastian. What's your name?"

"Ah," I started to say, then furrowed my brows. "I don't remember."

I didn't know my name. It was stuck, right there but just out of reach. A headache thumped at my temples, and the street-lights above us swam in swirls as I swallowed hard. I closed my eyes and thought about the sky, the fresh Chinese take-away smell wafting in the air, and the ocean—we were nowhere near the ocean, but I smelled it, nevertheless. I swallowed again, chasing down the vomit—throwing up would not be a good idea, not with my pulse thudding behind my eyes.

"We need to take her to casualty." This from Sebastian's friend, who was walking beside him.

"She needs help urgently," Sebastian said. "She won't make the trip."

"If we drop her off at the medical center, they will not treat her. They aren't equipped to handle her condition properly." This was the first time the man who walked ahead had spoken.

I opened my eyes, but all I saw was his dark brown hair brushed close to his head and stayed in place as he glided onward. And he wore a beautiful luxury coat that flowed to his ankles and billowed behind him in mystery and intrigue.

Sebastian did his best to walk without hurting me, but every now and again pain shot up my left leg and dug deeply into my side. All the while, the headache burned through my brain. My blood was on fire as it moved through my veins, and I winced with each step Sebastian took. I didn't know if I could manage going any farther.

I cried out and grabbed my left-hand side. Flesh started tearing near my bellybutton and spine like I was being torn in two. I wondered whether my insides would exit the wound.

I didn't know what it was about this attack, but this didn't feel normal. Nothing about an attack was normal, but this, this was something else; the burning of my skin, the fire in my blood and the feel of my flesh as it kept tearing.

None of it was *normal*.

Sebastian moved me slightly in his arms so that he could gently lay his hand over mine as I held onto my side.

"We are almost at my master's place," he said gently. "Just one more block." He smiled, but there was sadness in his eyes.

I didn't know this kind man helping me and couldn't interpret his expressions but the tenderness of his touch, as comforting as it was, left me worried. Whatever had happened to me in that alley might be the death of me.

But if I was about to die, I needed something to take my mind off death, and tear my thoughts away from the pain.

I glanced up at Sebastian; I might as well admire the view. He was beautiful; his lips full and kissable, grass green eyes with slivers of gold running through them and long eyelashes. He had high cheekbones, a square jaw, and the ear that I could see was nicely shaped and sat neatly against his head. He had short blonde hair that was shaved at the sides and a little longer on top, so that you could just see the beginning of velvety curls. His hair so soft I wanted to run my fingers through it. But there was something else about him.

"Which animal are you?" I asked, barely audible; my speech came as more of a mumble.

This wasn't the best time to make idle chit-chat, but I desperately wanted to stop thinking about the pain while my blood ran hot. The only thing I could think of was to talk.

"I'm a were-leopard." He flashed a wholesome grin. "How did you know?"

I didn't answer him. My eyes were heavy, and I rested my head on his broad shoulders, but I think I smiled. I couldn't remember.

And then I died.

Okay, I didn't die. I passed out from all the blood loss. I awoke to bright lights above me, and someone tugging on my abdomen. My whole body shook as they pulled down. I tried to sit, but small hands came from behind the little curtain in front of me and pushed me back onto the table.

"Don't sit. I'm busy suturing your side." Big brown eyes commanded from behind a pair of glasses, and her mouth was hidden behind a mask.

"Léon, I need help. It's too much; it's too deep."

The doctor stopped pulling on me and turned around. I looked to the left to see who she was talking to, and it was the other man—the one who had walked in front. His name was Léon. That name rang familiar. I knew it from somewhere. Just like my name, it's sitting on the tip of my tongue, but I couldn't say it.

One moment Léon was across the room, the next he stood beside the doctor—so close I could lift my hand and touch him. Either he had used magic, or I was just slow; it could've been both. I did a slow blink trying to process this information and stared at him.

He was talking to the doctor, but he stared at me. I saw his mouth move but couldn't comprehend what he was saying. He had exquisite eyes; they were ocean blue. Eyes you could look at every day. The blue of water so deep that you could fall into and drown. The dark brown or black hair framed a pale face with high cheekbones and a strong jaw.

They were whispering under their breath. I didn't know why I wanted to do this, it's like you always want to do the thing you shouldn't because it's not a good idea, but it's what I did. I tried to move my right arm, but it was heavy. I lifted it and a block of wood came with it along with the drip. Someone came into my view from above and grabbed my arm to move it back into place.

"Don't move," he whispered near the shell of my ear as he moved hair out of my face. "Relax, we will take care of you."

I couldn't see who it was, but his voice was smooth and soothing as velvet, and I relaxed my arm in his.

"Give her another shot."

I noticed the doctor watching me, as was Léon. Both their faces were blank, devoid of any emotion or telltale signs of what they were really thinking.

Someone had their back to me and was tinkering with the drip. Another slow blink, and I closed my eyes.

Hard grinding sounds and heavy moving concrete stirred me awake. I did not understand what the sound was, but it felt like the earth or I were moving. My arm rested around someone's waist, and they were gently cupping my hand in theirs. Their skin was warm and smelled of the ocean, with just a hint of citrus. There was also the smell of leaves and grass mixed in somewhere. I snuggled my face against their back, and it felt so warm, so safe.

What did I do last night to wake in someone's bed? I tensed. Opening my eyes, I wanted to take my hand away, but he held onto my hand and started turning around to face me. I kept tugging on my arm to set it free, but he kept holding on as he turned around. My chest tightened as I held my breath. As he faced me, I recognized him. It was Sebastian, the man who had carried me. He smiled, and we were close enough that I could see how green his eyes were, even with the slivers of gold—they reminded me of eyes on black kitty cats, the color of true green without the gray hues that most green-eyed people had.

His intense stare made me avert my eyes to see if I was wearing anything. The sheet came up under my arms. It covered everything, but I peeked inside the covers to see if I was naked —which I was, except for underwear. Thank goodness I still had *something* on.

Why was he in bed with me? I hoped he wasn't naked. The sheet was tucked underneath him from turning around, so that all I could see was his naked chest and waist. I felt heat creep up my neck. His smile widened. I pulled the sheet higher and tucked it all around me.

"Why are you in bed with me—and please tell me you are not naked?"

"Don't worry, your virtue is safe." He chuckled. "We have great healing capabilities, not only for were-animals but for humans as well. We took turns lying with you."

Someone moved behind me, and a squeal sound escaped my lips.

She laughed and said, "I don't like women, sweetheart." She patted me on my shoulder. "How do you feel?" She sat up far enough so that I could see her face. She too wore underwear—a navy sports bra with black panties. She threw the covers off and climbed out the bed.

"I don't know how I feel. I don't feel any pain, I think." I frowned.

I laid flat on my back and made sure the duvet tucked in everywhere. I straightened my legs and flexed my toes; something tightened around my left thigh, and a small cry escaped my mouth. Stitches pulled when I stretched my legs. My arms were above the covers, and I felt my left-hand side. There was something covering the wound—I'd look when I was alone. I didn't want to lift the covers and flash anyone. I might have flashed when they put me in the bed, but as I wasn't awake, that didn't count.

I lifted my hand to my head and felt stitches above my left eye, and more stitches on the side of my head where a section of my hair had been shaved. I could hide the wound when my hair was loose. I was lucky to be alive.

I watched the woman pull on jeans and a black t-shirt. She added a shoulder holster and put her gun in place. I tensed when she caught my eye.

"We are guards for the master." She answered my question without having to be asked, and she patted her gun like it was a pet.

"Which animal are you?" I said, my eyes flitting from her gun to her face.

She sat on the edge of the bed and pulled on socks and shoes. "I'm a were-rat, and he's a were-leopard." She pointed to Sebastian.

Okay, now I remembered Sebastian telling me he was a were-leopard when he carried me.

"Can you remember anything?" Sebastian asked.

I faced him. Sebastian had moved and sat against the headboard.

"No," I said, shaking my head at the same time—it didn't hurt. Yay for me! "How long have I been here?"

"Two days."

"Shit. Has it been *two days*? They ripped me to shreds, and I almost died. How come I feel so good? I shouldn't be feeling *this* good, should I?"

"Like I said, we are good at healing." Sebastian's smile reached his stunning green eyes, the color of fresh green leaves after a summer's rain.

"I don't suppose you know which were-animal attacked me and whether I will change into something furry at the next full moon?"

The two guards shared a look, but Sebastian answered. "We don't know. The doctor will take blood in a day or two for testing, and we will see at the end of the month if there are any," — he hesitated, perhaps trying to find the right word, — "*changes.*"

"Do you know if anyone has been looking for me? I should probably go to the police."

"Well, sweetheart," the were-rat stood and combed her fingers through her short brown hair, styled in a bob. "I think the police already have enough cases, and your file might fall to the bottom of their shit-list. Don't take this personally, but you might have to figure this one out on your own."

She must have seen the shock on my face and added, "I'm Elena." She smiled. To Sebastian she said, "Hang back and give her the in's and out's of everything; I'm sure they will fetch her for dinner later, or you can take her there yourself if you aren't busy." She waved goodbye and left.

Sebastian moved beside me and pulled the sheet off completely, revealing low hanging boxers. He had broad shoulders and a slim waist beneath a well-developed inguinal crease. He caught me staring, and I felt heat rise up my neck and face. He grinned mischievously and grabbed his clothing from a table.

I frowned with a hint of anger just below the surface; I guessed it's easier to be angry than embarrassed.

As if he knew I was still watching, Sebastian pulled his black jeans and t-shirt on seductively, and slow enough so that I could see all his muscles move. I licked dry lips. He wore a similar uniform to Elena.

Sebastian went to a shelf on the far wall and came back with a heap of clothing and toiletries which he placed on the bed near to me.

"We had to cut your old clothing from your body. Fortunately, the master arranged for new clothes for you. The bathroom is there," — he pointed to a door on his left, — "the doctor said you can shower with the plasters on." I nodded, feeling the dirt caked on my body, I needed a shower desperately. "I'll wait for you to freshen up so take your time, and then I'll take you to the kitchen for something to eat."

"Thank you," I said, pulling the sheet out from where it was tucked under the mattress and bunched it around my body like a large fluffy dress. Climbing off the bed was difficult with the sheet, but I tried to be as ladylike as I could whilst grabbing the pile of items with my free hand.

"Thank you for helping me back there in the alley. And for carrying me, and now for this; for healing me."

"It was nothing."

"Really? You save me, and it's nothing?"

"Why not?" His face was pleasant. There was no malice hidden there, only an honest face, clean shaven and almost inno-cent-looking. "We helped you because we could."

We held eye contact for a few seconds, and then I asked, "Who is this master you two keep referring to?"

"Léon. Does his name ring a bell?"

I shook my head. "Only from two nights ago, when you found me. But I don't really remember."

"He is the master of all the were-animals and vampires in Sterling Meadow."

I shrugged. The attack had taken the memory of who I was and everything else I knew before two days ago. I remembered Sterling Meadow, how to walk and talk. I knew which day it was but I didn't know who I was and I didn't know Léon.

The thought of not knowing left me frustrated. I was a shell of my former self, desperately needing to piece the puzzle of my life back together again.

If the police weren't able to help, would Léon or Sebastian? They didn't know me, and they didn't owe me anything, so why should they help me? I already owed them my life.

Now that Léon had gone out of his way to help me, I didn't

know if he wanted something in return. Did I owe him a favor now? If I did, what would that favor entail? Vampires schemed and plotted and used their power against each other. Their eyes alone could control humans. I didn't know what I'd do if Léon wanted to control *me*.

I was standing with the sheet around my body and clutching the items in my hands. Fatigue enveloped me and all I wanted to do was clean up before I became lethargic. "Okay," I said, my throat dry. "Let me shower quickly so we can eat," I said when my stomach grumbled.

I locked the bathroom door and placed the clothing and toiletries beside the neatly rolled white towels on the white marble table near the bath. The tiles all around, cream with dark swirls on them, made the walls come alive as you walked into the bathroom. The basin, toilet, and bath were black—a stark contrast to the usual white or cream. The shower could fit at least six people with enough jets to massage all your aching muscles at the same time, and the bath could seat at least four adults comfortably. The bathroom was huge and dark, but the colors blended well.

One wall was entirely dominated by mirrored glass, so that whatever you did in the shower or bath was in full view of anyone you shared the room with. I glanced at the mirror. I didn't want to see the damage, but I had to look.

I faced the mirror and dropped the sheet. I stared at my body. The three deep lines running across my left thigh had been stitched neatly. It must've been a large claw of a were-predator to cause that kind of damage.

I touched my abdomen lightly. I felt all the stitches through the large plaster that covered from my bellybutton all the way around to near my spine. Still trailing lightly along the edge of the plaster, near my pelvis, was a scar running up my abdomen.

It was a low vertical caesarian section scar that was old and didn't hurt when I ran my fingers over it. Doctors didn't take procedures like that lightly; the baby I'd carried had to come out immediately.

With everything that had happened, I hadn't thought of anything else. There was a possibility that, somewhere, I had a child waiting for me, and that I was married or lived with someone.

Something tightened in my chest. There could be someone waiting for me to come home. They might *need* me to come home.

Shit.

I twisted my body around so that I could see the full length of the large plaster and saw a tattoo of a butterfly—a Ulysses butterfly. Not a small dainty one on a shoulder, but a large 3D version with a wingspan of at least four inches on each shoulder blade. It was beautiful. It looked as though the butterfly could take flight from my back. The wings were shaded with bright blues and greens, and as I neared the mirror to see the detail, I saw each wing had been finely tattooed with intricate details that must have taken days to complete. The outline of the wings looked like hieroglyphic symbols, so small that the artist must have used the smallest needle possible, which came with a lot of pain.

It was hard to believe that this was who I was, a tattooed mother running around the streets at night. Alone.

I combed my fingers through my hair until I found the shaved section. It didn't hurt; surely, I should feel some pain? The stitches felt spiky against my fingertips as they brushed the smooth, naked skin surrounding it. My green eyes dark and were very close to a gray or charcoal color. My left eye socket and cheek were bruised, and already changing color like blossoming flowers in spring. The stitches above my eye were finer, and their immaculate presentation suggested that they might not leave a scar at all.

I should be dead with this amount of injury. I was not a were-animal or a vampire, and I didn't have any mystical powers. It was impossible that I had survived, and yet I had.

The confusion I felt was more than I could bear. I must've hit my head pretty hard not to be able to remember anything, and I needed to understand why I was alone in that alley.

A headache started, and I didn't want to think anymore.

With great care, I removed the underwear that I had awoken wearing, unsuccessfully trying to avoid any stabs of pain from my wounds. As I stood there naked in the unfamiliar bathroom, the true nature of the ordeal that I had sustained tore through me.

I climbed into the hot shower and cried. I let the tears flow down my face and mix with the hot water. I stood where no-one could hear or see me, and I held myself. I shivered under the hot water as it fell on my skin, and it felt good; I felt alive.

When I was ready to wash, I glanced at all the expensive-looking bottles standing on the glass shelves against the wall in the shower. The shampoo was French, as was the conditioner, and I used both to wash the traces of red from my long brown hair. As the water ran through it, my hair felt smooth and smelled fresh, vaguely reminding me of the scent of the ocean. The delicate and clean soap, also from France, had hints of citrus, lavender, and plum. I washed my body with the soap, and the foam cleaned all the dried blood away from my aching body.

My muscles didn't ache as much when I climbed out of the shower. It was only the sharp pull of the stitches in my skin that burned when I moved.

As drops of water ran along the contours of my body, I began to dry myself with one of the large towels from the table, wrapping it around my body so that it hung all the way to my shins.

Once dry, I took the toiletries from the table and set them near the basin. I brushed my teeth, applied some deodorant and used the face cream that was standing near the mirror beside the other little bottles. I rolled my eyes. I couldn't help but notice that *all* the cosmetics were French. I guessed that it was true what people said about vampires; some were unnecessarily elegant.

I reached for the fresh clothing that I had left beside the bath. The bra was lace and matched the panties, both silky and expensive. The underwear I had previously worn was all cotton and didn't match. As I slipped them on, I realized that, apart from the fact that they fitted perfectly, they were strangely comfortable. The new jeans were a perfect fit to the curve of my hips and slender waist. The black v-neck t-shirt was just as comfortable, and luckily the lace bra I wore beneath wasn't push-up, so there was no cleavage showing.

I stared at my toned body in the new outfit and flexed my bicep muscles. As soon as I had, I smiled. I looked like one of the guards in my black shirt and jeans.

I opened the bathroom door and saw Sebastian sitting in the chair reading a book. He glanced at me and frowned.

"What?"

"Your hair," he chortled.

"Shit." As soon as he mentioned it, I realized that my unkempt hair was still sodden from the shower. I went back into the bathroom, bent my body forward and towel-dried it.

When I came up, Sebastian stood next to me, holding a spray bottle.

"Turn around."

I warily did as he asked, staring at him in the mirror as he sprayed the stuff onto my hair.

"It will keep your hair soft."

I picked up a comb, and it glided through my hair like a hot knife through butter. My hair began to straighten, and, as Sebastian had promised, it *was* soft.

"Is this your room?" I asked him

"No, it's the master's."

"Shit."

"You say 'shit' a lot." He grinned.

"Well, yeah. You might, too, if you were me. I feel like I have invaded the man's personal space, and now I've used all his products."

"Don't worry about it. The master is a very generous host. You're welcome to use anything you find." In the mirror's reflection, Sebastian smiled, and although the warmth there seemed genuine, I also saw glimpses of darkness behind the alluring green eyes. He held my gaze for a moment before he spoke again, turning for the door. "Come, let's go eat."

I followed Sebastian out.

Three

We traversed down a long corridor. There were other bedrooms on either side and at the end of the hall, a gym, unisex showers and lockers. Men walked to their lockers without a towel around their waists, and they didn't seem bothered in the slightest when they saw me.

We turned a corner, and the smell of food wafted upon the air. The aromatic smells were tantalizing, and my mouth began to water. We climbed a flight of stairs with an entrance ahead, a dining room to the left and the kitchen on the right. The kitchen was buzzing with black-clothed bodyguards, all armed and serious.

The presence of so many support staff confounded me. If the master was well liked, why did he need so many guards?

Near the kitchen's central island, guards walked around with plates, some empty and others filled with food. There were two chefs preparing the food, both dressed in their white uniforms, entirely focused on ensuring the quality of the evening's service.

Sebastian led me to the island and handed me a plate.

"They always serve three different proteins with carbs; meat, chicken, or veg. Cold drinks are over there in the fridge, but there is also coffee if you'd prefer." He pointed to the items and moved along the island toward the food. As the chefs moved near to us, he added, "The chefs are mute, but they hear everything, so be careful what you say here." He winked wickedly.

Sebastian nodded at them. They greeted him and turned to face me, offering a small bow. I wasn't sure what to do, so I simply nodded back.

We plated up our food choice and sat at a clean table near the back of the dining room, with our backs to the wall.

My plate had almost the same amount of food as Sebastian. The food looked delicious and smelled so divine that I had to try a bit of it all: lasagne, roast chicken breasts, a baked potato, and a salad on the side. I went back a second time to grab a bottle of water and a cup of coffee. We ate in comfortable silence as we watched the guards come and go.

My thoughts drifted toward the attack, and my rapid healing. If I had been healed by the were-animals' ability alone, then that was great. But I wondered if there was something else I should know about. Perhaps I was infected and would turn furry at the next full moon. If that was the case, which animal would I become? Which *beast*?

And, if I didn't shift, then I had to be a vampire. Vampires healed almost any injury; their throat could be ripped out, and they would still heal. A vampire need only bite a human without draining them, feed them their blood, then two days later, the human would wake, hungry for blood. I wasn't craving blood as far as I could tell, but that didn't mean I wasn't turning into one, either.

It was bordering on ridiculous, really. Of all the things I

couldn't remember—like my name—I remembered facts about vampires and were-animals.

As I sat lost in thought, Sebastian's plate became almost empty, whereas mine was only half-eaten. Despite my hunger, it hadn't taken long for me to realize that I couldn't eat it all. I pushed food around on my plate while I waited for him to finish, drinking a few sips of coffee before pushing it aside, along with the plate.

I couldn't escape my thoughts. That Sebastian and Léon must have done something different in order to save my life. More importantly, what did I have to do in return?

"Are you ready?"

I flinched when Sebastian spoke, even though his voice was pleasant.

"Sorry," he said, smiling. "I didn't mean to startle you." He had a luscious smile, all perfect teeth and full lips. "Are you ready?" He repeated.

"Lead the way," I said, pretending I didn't just stare at him again.

I followed him again, this time in the opposite direction. We climbed another flight of stairs toward an office, the walls of which were glass and tinted silver. Sebastian knocked on the glass door, and someone from within said, 'Enter'.

As Sebastian opened the door, all I could see was the wall to its left, covered from floor to ceiling in shelves that were each lined with books. From where I stood, their covers looked leathery and old. Inside the room were two sofas, a two-seater near to the door facing a one-seater directly opposite. To the far right sat an old wooden desk framed with wrought iron and, behind it, the man they called 'master'.

Léon sat perfectly still, showing no emotion. His dark brown hair fell loosely around his face, framing a square jaw, high cheekbones and ocean-deep eyes. I turned away from his stare to glance at the rest of his office.

"Don't worry, I won't roll your mind with my eyes. You have my word," Léon said with humor.

I looked at him again and felt nothing from the vampire. There was no pull or metaphysical attachment, just him, Sebastian and I in a quiet room.

"That will be all, Sebastian. You may wait for her outside. And please close the door."

"Sure," Sebastian muttered, leaving the room.

When we were alone, Léon walked around his desk to sit on its edge and crossed his arms over his chest. He wore a blue-collar silk shirt that gaped slightly to reveal a smooth chest, dark blue jeans and boots. He dressed very modern for a master vampire.

There was only silence between us as he gazed at me. His glare had a weight to it, so intense that I felt I could slice through it with a knife. The hairs along my neck and back stood on end, and I shivered. I tried crossing my arms defensively before eventually leaving them to hang loose by my sides.

To fill the silence, I said, "Thank you for saving my life."

He nodded, stretching the silence out for a second, and then said, "I'm happy to see how well you have recovered. My were-animals did a fantastic job." He uncrossed his arms and rested them on his legs. "Are you in any pain?"

"Not really, except for where the skin is pulled tight by the stitches." I reached for my side to feel the plaster under my shirt and the stitches beneath it. "I don't know how you did it but I should be dead, shouldn't I?"

"Yes, you should be."

"Did you make me?" I didn't know how to say it, so I

decided it was probably best to just get it out. "What I mean is, did you turn me into a vampire?"

The corners of his mouth tilted upward as if wanting to laugh, but Léon stopped when he saw my face.

"No, I wouldn't do such a thing to someone who was unconscious," he said. "If it was something you wanted, I would do it, but it has to be *your* choice." His voice was stern yet smooth. Something in the way he said it sounded like he had not been given the choice at the time of his transformation, or he had known someone in that situation.

"Then what did you do to me?" I asked, sounding accusatory and a little angry. I breathed deeply before I said anything else that sounded either harsh or unappreciative.

"Come." He motioned for us to sit on the sofas. "Let's sit."

His cold, long fingers curled around my elbow and guided me to the two-seater. His touch was delicate yet firm, and he smelled faintly of the ocean, no doubt from the same soap that I had used in his shower. His cologne was fresh and sharp, with an undertone of cedarwood.

As he sat down beside me, Léon pulled on his shirt and tugged his pants down until he was comfortable in the seat. "Your wounds were very serious," he said. "You were dying. When Mel realized that we were out of options and you were near death, she suggested something other than vampirism." He paused, waiting for my reaction.

He didn't have to explain, but Mel must have been the female doctor who had tended to me.

"Am I going to get upset when you tell me?"

"You might." He shrugged and glanced at the far wall. "And, as you can see, I'm having difficulty explaining it to you. I don't know how you will handle it. It's not something that any normal human wants."

"Just say it. I know I was at death's door. There was little you could do." It was true—I had been dying. My attackers had pulled me apart, and only a miracle could heal me.

"Right." He reverted to what I felt was a vampire posture, as though his face and body were carved from stone. He glanced at me with his drowning blue eyes. "I marked you."

"What does that mean? You *marked* me?"

"In my world, there are vampires, then were-animals, then humans, and lastly, pets which we use for food. A vampire can take one or more of each if they so desire and mark them. They become an extension of the vampire and may increase the vampire's power base. I marked you to be my human servant. I offered you a lifeline, an extension of my power that healed you."

My smile wavered, my head shaking as his words reverberated within my bones. I knew what a human servant was. I understood the concept. But the chill of the realization made me uncomfortably numb. The only way to save my life had been to *mark* me.

I didn't understand what it meant for me going forward. My eyes flitted to Léon and I wondered what it would mean to him.

I hugged myself and touched my side, rubbing lightly over the stitches through the plaster and my clothing. Maybe I needed some pain to help me think, but all it did was tickle and irritate the tender flesh.

None of my thoughts gave me comfort. All I had left was to ask Léon for guidance. "What exactly does that mean for me?"

"It means you are my human servant. Please trust me when I tell you that I only did it to save your life. I will not give you the second mark. You will not become my full human servant. I won't do that to you." He smiled, intending to be reassuring.

"We will help you find out who you are and then you can go home. We do not have to see each other again."

My mouth opened, but I couldn't think of anything to say. I felt the lines between my eyes deepen as I frowned. He had saved my life and claimed to want nothing in return, and yet, I was forever bound to him. We were bound to each other until one of us died or was killed, and with Léon being a vampire, it seemed unlikely that I would be the one to survive the arrangement.

There had to be a catch.

"Just like that, you're letting me go?" I said, narrowing my eyes. He gave a slight bow of his head. "What kind of power will you have over me?"

"One mark is not much," he said, pulling his sleeves down one at a time. "It was enough to share my life essence with you, and that is what saved you. But since you do not possess any powers yourself, you have nothing to offer me. I do not think it would be necessary for us to keep in contact—unless you are offering your blood to me?"

He studied me carefully, like he was waiting for me to freak out. I stared at him while my mind buzzed. I'm certain my face was blank; a face that held no emotion, one that I could hide behind while I considered what he said to me. I couldn't believe it. Was he actually going to let me go after saving me?

If I remembered correctly, vampires typically weren't this generous. Ever. He received nothing out of this arrangement. Absolutely *nothing*.

"I'm sorry. It seems like you got a raw deal."

"Yes, so it seems," he said. His smile reached his eyes, and I saw a flash of fangs.

"Shit." I sat back, and leaned my head against the seat and closed my eyes. "Have you ever had a human servant before?"

"No, you are the first."

"How old are you, and why haven't you had a human servant before?"

I guess that bothered me more than I realized. I couldn't understand why he hadn't turned anyone into a human servant before me. I didn't know him, so I didn't have any insight into the type of vampire he was, but he seemed to be like no other. Perhaps he was so powerful that he didn't need one.

"You get straight to the point, don't you?" He turned to face me, and I noticed he did so without putting his neck at an odd angle. Could vampires get a crick in the neck?

"It's new to me, too. Heaven knows what will fly out of my mouth next."

"Fair enough," he said with a hint of a grin. "I'm over eight hundred years old, and I've never had a reason to make any human my servant. I don't need one, but this was necessary." He waved his hands in my direction.

"Will anything happen to you if I die?"

"Maybe. But with one mark, again, I can't be sure."

"You don't know me, yet you saved me and ended up with someone you don't need. If anything happens to me, you might get hurt."

He shrugged modestly. "You were dying."

"Are you going to want something in return?" I wiped damp hands on my jeans and felt my t-shirt cling to my body. I hoped I didn't have to do *things* for him.

"No, I want nothing in return. Well, perhaps one thing—that you tell *no-one* of our arrangement." His eyebrows arched, and something similar to panic flashed in his eyes.

At least that was something I could live with. "Sure," I said, relieved. I would take this to my grave.

"Besides, Mel informed me that you may have a child somewhere, and I would never tear a parent away from their children. *Ever.* I may be many things, but I am not that kind of monster."

Ah, he knew. Obviously his doctor told him everything. And he was a monster with feelings. Interesting.

There was one more thing I needed to know. "The bites. Do you know whether I will turn into a were-animal come full moon?" Since Léon made me his human servant, I didn't think I'd turn into a were-animal but I needed to know.

"No, we don't think so, but Mel will run more tests, just to be sure." He stood and walked back to his desk. "I have assigned Sebastian to you until you figure everything out. All my resources are at your disposal."

"Thank you." I sensed that our conversation was coming to a close. I rose and headed for the door. "You have been very generous, Léon. If you need your room back, I can sleep anywhere there is an empty bed. I don't expect you to give up your room for me."

"No, you can use it." He was already going through documents on his desk.

"Will your girlfriend, wife, or significant other not want to stay there with you?"

"No need, the room is yours for as long as you like. Although I may have to use the bathroom once in a while." His answer revealed nothing and I thought it best not to bother him with more questions.

I opened the door. "Thank you again."

He didn't answer as I left. Out in the hallway, Sebastian leaned against the wall with his arms behind his back, one knee bent and his foot against the wall.

"You ready?" he asked as he pushed himself away from the wall.

"For what?"

"I thought we could go to the alley where we found you. Perhaps you dropped a bag or something."

"Ah, not just a pretty face." I regretted the words the moment they flew out of my mouth.

He grinned. "Do you always flirt with the help?"

I choked on spit. "Sorry, I seem to say what I think and it was too good a comment to pass up."

"So I've noticed." Still smiling, Sebastian pointed back toward the stairs. "Let's go."

Four

I followed Sebastian the way we had come, but he stopped at a door to the right; we went through it and along a dark corridor, through a second door, and then we were outside. The door closed behind us, but there was no handle. Good to know; I could exit, but couldn't get back in again. I surveyed the area and couldn't see any other doors along the walls.

"Where's the entrance to get back inside?" I asked, pointing at the door we'd just exited.

"It's around the other side. You will see it when we return."

It was night, and the air had a slight breeze, but it was comfortably warm. It didn't feel late, but I wanted to know what the time was. I asked Sebastian. He glanced at his watch and said it was 20:30; it felt later than that.

I had been asleep for two days and woke up in a building with no windows, which left me feeling disorientated and with no sense of time. I should have realized it was night-time because Léon was awake, vampires only graced us with their presence after dark.

It made me wonder whether I was always this slow, or if I was still reeling from the after-effects of the attack. I didn't want to dwell too much on it and instead tried to enjoy the walk.

We traversed a few blocks in silence, the knot in my stomach pulling tighter and sweat beading on my forehead.

There were buildings on either side of the street. The side we walked on had apartment buildings, while the other had shops. We crossed the street and headed for the shops.

As we neared a dark opening just before the shops, I froze.

Sebastian entered the gloomy alley and was near the dumpster before realizing I wasn't alongside him. He looked over his shoulder, saw that I was still by the entrance and walked back.

"Are you all right?" he asked, lifting his hand to touch my shoulder but stopping mid-air.

Even though I was shivering, my clothing clung to my body. Near the wall was a large, dark pool of dried blood. The smell of metal and rotting meat burned my nose. Tears stung my cheeks. I staggered to the side, hunched my shoulders and leaned against the corner of the wall.

Sebastian touched the arm not against the wall and gently rubbed like one would to console a child.

The sharp ache moved along my spine, from my stomach into my chest. My breathing labored. I pressed my head against the wall until it hurt. I looked away and slid down the wall onto my haunches.

Sebastian crouched beside me and cupped one side of my face. "I will look around. Call me if you need me."

He left me in a huddle of despair as he searched around the alley. His flashlight was on, and he started moving boxes around, kicked old rags out of the way, and pushed the dumpster from the wall after looking inside.

Blood rushed in my ears and my pulse sped up. I felt like an animal trapped in a snare. I didn't want to see anything more, so I scooted onto the pavement with my back against the wall, away from the alley and closer to the laundromat next door. I could see my surroundings under the fluorescent lights, and I inhaled deeply and exhaled slowly. The beating of my heart against my chest began to ease, and I could once more focus on the street in front of me.

People walked along the pavement, minding their own business like I wasn't there. I was glad; I would hate for someone to throw a coin my way or ask if I was lost. The road was busy as cars drove up and down, but it was just like any other road.

My legs weren't stable enough for me to stand, so I went onto all fours and crawled forward a little. I glanced to the right to see what other shops were open. The first shop was a laundromat, then Mr. Ming's Chinese restaurant, a convenience store, and, at the far end, a hair salon. Above the stores were apartments. I glanced up at the lights between Mr. Ming's and the convenience store and saw two cameras, both pointing in opposite directions along the street.

"There is nothing else back there."

I flinched and clutched at my chest. Sebastian had stepped out of the alley and towered above me in the night air. "Jesus! You don't have to sneak up on me like that."

"Sorry, I didn't mean to startle you." He held out his hand. "I found these."

I stared up at him and saw keys dangling from a key chain. I needed to stand, but my legs felt like Jell-O. I crawled back to the wall, and used it to stand and leaned against it.

"What are those markings?" I asked, squinting at the keys as I reached for them.

"They look like hieroglyphics."

I took them from him. "Do you think these are mine?"

He shrugged. "Maybe."

The hieroglyphic markings on the key chain reminded me of the large Ulysses butterfly tattoo across my shoulders. They were reminiscent of the intricate hieroglyphics outlining the butterfly and embedded in its wings.

Maybe they were my house keys, but then again, maybe not.

There were three keys attached to the key chain, and none looked like your usual house key. All three keys were old and rusty. The first one was just the shape of a long 'L', while the top had three loops next to each other and a loop above them, like a crown. The second was shaped like the legs of a bar stool. The top had three loops surrounding one loop; also a crown, but plainer. The third was beautiful; its shape was like nothing I'd ever seen. The bit looked intricate, and the bow was a complicated crown; I couldn't describe it. Picture the biggest and prettiest crown a queen would wear, and that's what it looked like.

"It could be mine," I said.

"Yeah, when I saw the hieroglyphics, they reminded me of your tattoo."

I didn't look at him when he said that; I felt heat rush up my neck. Had everyone seen the Ulysses butterfly tattoo?

"Maybe keep them in case."

I slipped them into my jean pocket.

"I saw cameras over there." I pointed to where they were. "Maybe we should find out who monitors them? Maybe we can see something from that night?"

We went inside the laundromat and found it empty; it was a

self-service laundromat with a few vending machines against the wall.

Next we tried Mr. Ming's and found Bartholomew behind the till—at least, that's what his name tag read. Nah, ordering Chinese food from Bartholomew just didn't sound right. He promised us it was the best in town. I didn't believe him, and neither did Sebastian. Bartholomew didn't know who managed the cameras and said to try the convenience store.

The convenience store was larger than the previous two premises. It had six rows of shelves filled with convenience food in neat packaging and fridges at the back. Sebastian walked through the rows. I assumed he wanted to see if there was anyone else inside the store.

I stood at the check-out and cleared my throat until the cashier paid me attention.

He looked up from his phone and said, "Can I help you?"

"Do you know who manages the cameras outside?" I pointed to the cameras that sat outside the window.

"Who wants to know?" he asked, his lips smacking together as he chewed bubble gum.

"*We* do." I gave him my best dead-eyes. His attitude didn't disturb me; I could give plenty of attitude back.

"Did something happen?" he asked, as he made a snorting sound from the back of his throat and swallowed.

I shuddered; that was disgusting.

"Yes, now can you help us or not?" I was losing patience but tried not to sound too hostile; we needed his help if the cameras belonged to this shop.

"Sure, sure—just chill," he said. His name was embroidered on his shirt, and it read, 'Gus'.

"Thanks, Gus." I said, forcing a smile I knew wasn't friendly, but he ignored me and moved around the counter.

I wasn't clued up on police procedures, but I was sure we needed some kind of paperwork giving us permission to view their videos. I didn't think he was the sharpest pencil in the box and we didn't mind the help, so we continued as if nothing was out of the ordinary.

Gus led us toward the back of the store and opened one door. "We record for one week and then record over the previous week's footage. Just leave the door open in case the manager comes back."

"Thanks," Sebastian said, entering first.

Sebastian sat on the chair and started pressing buttons, and one of the little televisions started rewinding. I stood behind him trying to see what he was doing and how he was doing it but gave up and watched the little monitor instead.

There were date and time stamps at the bottom left-hand corner of the monitor, and Sebastian stopped the film a day before I was attacked and fast forwarded. The video wasn't going fast enough that we couldn't make out people's faces. It was a high-definition camera, and the video was clear at that speed. Three men walked along the pavement that night and stopped near the alley, two men moving out of view and, moments later, one man appeared carrying someone—me.

There was no video of me arriving, only being carried out.

When the time stamp reached today with the two of us walking into the store, we knew that I hadn't entered the alley from the street side.

"Shit. How did I get in the alley if I didn't come from the street?"

"From the park side." Sebastian stood. "Come on, let's go through the entrance next to the hair salon."

We thanked Gus and left.

The entrance that led us to the park was cleaner than the

alley, and the gate was unlocked. The park was large, with playground equipment for kids to play on and plenty of trees that were high enough and big enough to cast large areas of shade for picnics. There were lamp posts scattered around the park that illuminated the play area and cast shadows across the grass. My shoes sank into the soft, wet ground.

We walked along the brick wall of the building until we reached the spot where we thought the alley would be. On the ground was a wooden box pushed right up against the wall, with fresh scratch marks going up and over it.

"Let's see if you are able to climb up." Sebastian motioned for me to go closer to the wall.

I hesitated with one foot on the wooden box and tested it to see whether it would hold my weight. It did. I lifted my arms to reach the top of the wall and held onto the ledge, but, when I tried lifting myself up, pain tore through my abdomen and I cried out, letting go of the wall.

Sebastian caught me before I hit the ground. "You okay?" He held onto me until I could stand unaided.

"I'm fine," I snapped, pulling my shirt down. I wasn't angry at him, but at myself for the situation I was in.

"Let's go this way." Sebastian ignored my retort and pointed toward the hill on the far side of the park. "You must have come through the entrance over there."

I followed Sebastian along the footpath through the park. It was a beautiful evening for a stroll and I admired the view in front of me; his body moved like liquid metal, smooth and limber.

The rhythmic chirping of crickets sounded in the distance. The evening sky, with its same twinkling stars, reminded me of the cold ground I had woken up only a few nights ago. Autumn was only a month away, and the cool wind was pleasant. The smell of wet leaves and freshly cut grass played along my nose as we walked along the path. The park would be enjoyable during the day, with the warm sun on your face and being able to bask in the sounds of laughter.

We came around a small hill and reached the beginning of the forest. Ahead, there was a jetty from which people could take their boats out to fish. There was a hiking trail that led deep into the forest with an assortment of color-coded signs showing various paths. There was only one car in the parking lot. As we approached it, I saw the car was covered in a thin layer of debris.

"Let's check it out," Sebastian said, leading the way.

It was an old blue Honda; the exterior was still in good condition and immaculate inside. Sebastian tried the driver's side door, but it was locked. I tried the other side, and the back door opened. I looked up at him and smiled. No alarms went off, and it didn't look like anything scary would jump out. The back seat was clean, empty, with nothing in the pockets behind the front seats. I felt under the seat and came away with a parking stub for a dance club called 'Kiss'.

I held the stub out for him to see. "Do you know a place called 'Kiss'?"

His eyes widened and his expression changed, "Yes, I know it. It's where everyone goes to dance with the vampires," he said with a bitter undertone.

I didn't know whether to probe so thought it best to keep quiet while he went around to the back of the car and tried the trunk. It opened.

I crawled into the passenger's seat to open the glove compartment but found it empty; there was no pink slip, no license, no mail; just a map book of the city with a bookmark. I opened the map book to the page where the bookmark was, and it showed the street view of the little shops and apartment buildings surrounding the alley where I was found. It also focused on the park. There was a large red circle around everything.

Shit!

It took me a moment to realize what I was looking at, I frowned and wished I hadn't. Pain pierced between my eyes, and I started massaging my forehead and eye sockets with my thumbs.

I pulled the door handle, but it was locked. I tried the handle again, and it was still locked. I flicked the latch until the red square didn't show and pulled the handle to open it. As I started to step out, my foot caught on the lip of the carpet and I fell out of the car, landing on my knees on the concrete. I yelled "Ow!" and started rubbing my knees.

When I glanced at Sebastian, he was standing near the open trunk; his face pale and eyes wide. I wouldn't have thought someone like him would scare easily, but something in there had clearly got to him.

"What is it, Sebastian?" I stood and approached him slowly.

He lifted his hand and shook his head. I stopped.

"You don't want to see this." His green eyes seemed a shade lighter, and I saw more of the whites of his eyes.

There was something in there that I shouldn't see, but now I had to see. I was stubborn that way. "I have to see what's in the trunk, Sebastian. I found a map with a circle around this area. This has to be my car, and I need to know what the *fuck* is going on."

I heard him swallow. "Trust me. You don't want to see this."

"I'm coming to have a look." I stomped my feet toward the open trunk, and the smell of rotting meat took my breath away.

I stood beside Sebastian and stared at the contents. I saw something inside, but I couldn't quite understand exactly *what* I was looking at. My mind was trying to protect me from the horror in the trunk. There was a tarp stained maroon by something wrapped within it. Sebastian pulled the tarp open.

I blinked, but I was slow to process what I was seeing. Once I saw it, I could no longer unsee it, and, for that, I would suffer from a shit load of nightmares.

Something on the tarp moved through the thick black goo. At night, blood appeared dark, which I had to admit was a relief. I squinted and eventually saw little white maggots crawling through it, over and around the tarp. There were even little black bugs and flies. The thing wrapped in the tarp was bloody and missing pieces. The pale skin of a man's torso. His arms, legs and groin all torn or bitten off—I couldn't tell. I didn't know.

I didn't *want* to know.

On his pectoral muscle above the left nipple was a tattoo of a Ulysses butterfly, with the same blue and green wings as on my back. It was also a 3D Ulysses butterfly and looked considerably more alive than the man, as though it was resting on his body and about to fly away. The tattoo had similar hieroglyphic detail as the one on my back, but it was smaller; I wasn't sure, but I also didn't want to get up close and check.

The smell of rotting flesh and dried blood filled my nostrils, and I felt my dinner was about to come back out. I ran as far away as I could before the vomit came. My head hurt as I hunched over the wet grass, vomiting again and again, until I had nothing more to throw up. I wiped my mouth with the back of my hand and stood straight.

Fuck. My body either reacted to the smell from the trunk or to the fact that I must have known the person lying in the trunk of my car. I didn't want to cry again this evening, but dammit, I couldn't help it. Tears stung my cheeks. I heard Sebastian talking to someone on his cellphone, but I couldn't hear what he was saying. I only heard the catch in my breath and the rush of blood pumping in my ears.

I didn't want to look at the car or at Sebastian. I looked everywhere else, and there was nothing else around us except nature. Nature was good. Nature was pleasant. It was a place where people could go on hikes through the forest or take a boat out on the water. A park where kids could play. It was a lovely family area to do fun things in; not for anyone to find a dead body.

I inhaled and exhaled slowly, trying to concentrate on my breathing and wiping the last of the tears away. I let out a slow, shaky breath, and the tears stopped.

Was someone trying to kill me and the people I knew?

Are the butterfly tattoos important, or just something I shared with that man in the trunk?

Who did I work for, and where did I live?

I only had questions. Definitely no answers.

My breath came quick and shallow, and my hands clutched my chest. I thought I'd been doing so well with the controlled breathing.

I stared out across the water and saw the fog roll in, getting closer to me. The trees from the forest swayed as the faint wind blew threw their branches. I couldn't comprehend what was happening around me.

I thought too much; my chest ached, and my head felt foggy. My eyes closed, and I fell. All I knew as I fell was that I was glad the darkness swallowed me whole.

Five

I awoke to find that I was lying in a Victorian bath, water lapping gently up to my neck. The soapsuds felt soft and silky against my skin, and there was the scent of lavender and roses in the air. The fragrant aroma was a comfort as I closed my eyes and drifted off to the soft melody of a harp.

A splash brought me back to my surroundings. Tiny bubbles escaped the water near my knees. The dark curve of something sharp yet round rose slowly out of the water.

I thought *snake*.

I reached for it, expecting its surface to be smooth and glossy as the skin of a snake would be, but instead it was hard and coarse. I held on, trying to get it away from me. More of the object rose out of the water, and its black claws reached for me and slashed my face. I hit and kicked those black claws away from me.

"Jesus, woman— *calm down*. It was just a dream." I recognized Elena's voice.

I was in bed, Elena was straddling my waist and keeping my

wrists above my head and away from her. I relaxed in her vise grip. She held her position for a moment then when she realized I wasn't struggling she climbed off.

"Those claws felt so real; they were coming at me. I had to stop it from hurting me." I choked back a sob. "What happened? Why were you on me?"

"You fainted at the park, and when they brought you back, Mel changed your dressings and found your stitches had split. She stitched you back together, and I took the first shift to lie beside you."

"Shit. Thank you. Sorry for attacking you. Did I hurt you?"

"Don't sweat it, girl." Her eyes flitted to her forearms; there were bloody trail marks from where I had embedded my nails as we had grabbled. "I needed to get up, anyway. Change of guards and all that," she smiled and started pulling on black jeans.

"Don't you guys wear anything else besides black?"

"Ha-ha. Don't you know that the number one rule of guarding is to always wear black?" She gave me a two-finger salute and pulled on her black t-shirt. This one had a logo above her left breast, an open mouth with a pair of fangs. It looked like it would take a bite out of her breast.

"Where are you working?" I asked, pointing at the logo.

"At one of the master's clubs. He has everybody working on rotation, so each day we work somewhere else."

"What is it called? How many clubs does he have?"

She stopped what she was doing and gave me her attention. "You know the master owns a lot of businesses, right? Besides the clubs, he has a few buildings and apartment blocks with a shitload of people working for him." She sounded tired when she said that and I wondered if she ever took vacation days.

"I do now." I sighed and pulled the sheets over my chest, tucking them under my body.

"He hired a private investigator to help you, especially after you guys found that body in the car last night."

"Fuck, I forgot about that. I'm a terrible person." How could I forget seeing that grisly sight?

Elena smiled reassuringly. "Stop beating yourself up; you've gone through enough trauma. You need to try and relax. Maybe if you didn't stress so much about it, your memory might return. Usually when I stop thinking about something, that's when things click into place."

"Yeah, you're probably right."

"And, just so you know, the master is in the bathroom." She grinned as she said that. "I've got to go. Hang tight; Sebastian said he would be here soon."

"Thanks."

All I wanted to do was get dressed and get out. I was half-naked, in a vampire's bed, and I didn't want to be here when he finished in the bathroom. I tried listening to what he was doing but couldn't hear a thing. Perhaps his bathroom was sound-proofed.

I scanned the room for clothing, but there wasn't any. If I didn't have any clothes, I would have to stay in bed. I turned to face the wall away from the bathroom door and tucked the pillow under my neck until I was comfortable.

There was something missing; the sheets were cold. I was missing Elena's heat, her warm body beside mine. As the silk sheets finally warmed against my skin, I closed my eyes and drifted off to sleep.

A heavy, metallic sound began grinding against concrete and the walls shifted. As the sounds vibrated through the walls, there was a slight movement on the bed. I rolled over to see what it was and caught sight of Léon's back. He was wearing a black shirt with a high collar and dark blue jeans. He was pulling on boots.

"How are you feeling?" he asked, without turning around.

I tensed, forgetting he could hear me move in the next room so the chances of him hearing the change in my breathing when I awoke were great.

"I guess I'm fine, considering." I tucked the sheet between my face and the pillow and wanted—no, *needed*—a teddy bear or something soft to cuddle against me in the sheets. My sanity depended on it.

He laughed.

I frowned.

"Sorry; when I'm near someone, I can hear whispers of their thoughts, like soft music playing in the background. I don't normally tune in, but I heard yours for a second. I will see what I can do about getting you a plush toy for your slumber."

I felt heat creep up my neck and cheeks.

"You know exactly what to say to a woman, don't you." I sounded grumpy even to myself. That was a private thought, and he tuned into my personal station.

His laughter felt like velvet rubbing against my skin, so soft. He turned to face me, and his smile reached his eyes as he hid his fangs. "I try."

There must have been a look on my face because he sobered quickly and said, "Are you all right?" He sat firmly against the headboard, crossed his legs by his ankles and folded his arms.

"I don't know."

"You're safe here."

"Were you reading my mind again?"

"No, it's the look on your face that tells me how scared you are. I employ a lot of were-animals to keep me and my people safe, and they will keep you safe, too."

"What if I'm the reason your people are no longer safe?"

He understood what I meant. What if I was the boogeyman? Or what if the boogeyman came here to kill me—or him? He leaned over and gently brushed hair out of my face.

"I have a private investigator looking into your shared Ulysses butterfly tattoo and whether it means anything, particularly in light of you sharing the same design with the corpse from the car. I hope you don't mind, but we took your fingerprints in the hope that it will speed up the process."

"What if the news is horrible? I don't know if I want to know."

"Cross that bridge when you get there." He shrugged as though it meant something and nothing at once, then added, "I'll be over at the club if you and Sebastian want to come over."

"Thanks, but I don't think I'm in the mood for a club. Besides, I don't have any clothes."

He smirked. "You have plenty of clothes." He climbed off the bed and opened a cupboard to reveal an array of women's clothing.

I sat up to look at the clothing and frowned. "Did you buy all those for me, or are they someone else's and they left them behind?"

"Elena bought them for you today. That way, you have a choice of items, and not just jeans and t-shirts." He glanced down at something on me, and I followed his line of sight. I pulled the sheets up to my neck, covering my breasts. My entire body was now hot.

"Well, if you change your mind, just let Sebastian know. He can be a lot of fun. Maybe you need a distraction to take your mind off the bad things."

"You are the second person to say that. If someone else suggests it, I will take it as a sign." I still sounded grumpy.

"Good." He paused for a second, opened his mouth and closed it again. There was something in his expression—maybe the lines between his eyes or the stillness of his body—that suggested there was something he wanted to say, but he didn't.

His ocean-blue eyes glistened, and it looked like there were tiny stars shining in them from where I was sitting. His stare was intense, almost as though he was trying to look deep inside my soul.

I blinked and turned away. "Is there anything you want to say to me?" I glanced at him again, matching his frown with my own.

"No, it's nothing." He left without another word, leaving me to wonder exactly what it was that he had wanted to say.

With the door closed, I climbed out of the bed, this time leaving the sheet. I showered until I once again smelled like an exotic French woman, and, with the towel wrapped around my body, I stood in front of the cupboard deciding what to wear now that I had all this new clothing.

There was a soft knock at the door and I yelled, "Who is it?"

"Sebastian."

"You can come in."

He opened the door and stopped halfway when he saw me. "You aren't dressed."

"Still deciding what to wear now that I have so much choice," I said, pointing at the clothing. "Don't you find it odd that Léon bought all these clothes for me? Like I would stay here for a while?"

"I have always known him to be generous."

"I'll say. I can't imagine all master vampires being like him. Have you met any others?"

"Yes." He didn't elaborate, and I didn't want to ask.

"What's the time?"

Sebastian glanced at his watch. "It's a little after 7p.m."

My mouth went slack. "I slept all day?"

"Uh-huh. You needed the rest."

"Léon told me about the private investigator." I remembered the corpse in the car and my shoulders sagged.

"Kit's good. We use him all the time. I'm sure he will find something."

"Especially now that he has my fingerprints."

Sebastian nodded quickly. "Yes, it will be quicker, and Kit has all the right connections." His expression softened, and a hint of sympathy entered his voice. "You were recently attacked, and someone cut up your friend. It wasn't your fault. We will find out what happened."

"We don't know that it wasn't my fault." My voice sounded strained. I bit my lip and blinked back tears.

He took a step toward me, but I backed away until I was against the bathroom door. He stayed where he was. I didn't want to be comforted; I wanted to feel anger instead of sadness. What I needed was to change the subject.

I swallowed hard and said. "What are we doing tonight?" I smiled, but the corners quivered.

"It's Friday. Almost everybody goes to the club."

I stared at his outfit; black jeans with a black dress shirt.

"Do you feel like going out?"

He shrugged. "Sure. Why not?"

I rolled my eyes. "I am not in my twenties. What do kids these days wear to clubs, anyway? And, by the way, you mustn't be a day older than twenty-five?"

His smile reached his eyes, now ablaze with a hint of mischief. "Twenty-eight."

I felt old. "Can you picture someone like *me* going clubbing?"

"You don't look a day over thirty," he said, walking to the cupboard and opened the other door.

There were more pants, more shirts, blouses, and a few dresses hanging within. He grabbed two hangers and handed them to me. "Wear this. I'll return in ten minutes."

I took the hangers from him and watched him leave. I held one hanger in my left hand and one in my right and lifted them. There was a black satin skirt and a shoe-string black lace top that required a black bra. I didn't know if I could trust a *guard*'s dress sense, but then again, he knew the vampire club, and this was probably the dress code. I grabbed black underwear and dressed.

There were still bruises and stitches on my face, but I wouldn't look too bad in a dark club. I walked out of the bathroom as Sebastian entered the room. As he saw me, his mouth gaped open.

"*Wow*. I didn't think you would wear it, but you look great."

"There wasn't really any other shoes, so the knee-high boots will have to do."

"No, it's great—it matches."

"You think the butterfly showing isn't too much?" I turned around to show him the rather large and obvious butterfly emblazoned on my back.

"It's a work of art. You shouldn't be embarrassed or feel ashamed. You have a jacket you can wear if you are cold," he said, grabbing a jacket out of the cupboard and handing it to me.

I pulled on the waist-length jacket to find it matched the outfit. I considered myself in the mirror, not feeling too uncomfortable in the lace and satin clothing, and without sounding self-centered—pleasing to the eye.

I followed Sebastian out of the room. Instead of heading along the straight corridor, we took a sharp left. I wanted to say something but thought I might have been mistaken. When I first came out of the room last night for dinner, we took a quick right and then passed the gym and lockers. I stopped and stared up the hallway we had just come from and down the one we were about to walk toward and knew I hadn't dreamt it. The hallway should be straight.

"Um, Sebastian?"

He stopped walking, and waited for me to finish my thought.

"I might be going crazy, but why do I think the walls and rooms moved?"

He grinned, flashing bright white teeth, and walked back to me. "That's because the walls and rooms do change. They rotate every twelve hours."

"Is that the noises I keep hearing?"

He nodded.

"Why?" I frowned; I had never heard of such a thing.

"To keep people from memorizing the layout of the building, and to ensure that should someone break in, they will most likely get lost."

"No shit. I am lost."

He held his hand out for me. "Not with me, you aren't."

I hesitated but took it.

"Léon has survived four attempts on his life and suspects it's the same people each time. He doesn't know who they are because the people they send after him tend to die before he can question them."

"You mean he kills them, don't you?"

"Yes."

"Why do they want him dead?"

"We have our suspicions." He didn't elaborate.

"But you don't want to talk about it."

"It's best if we don't."

"You seem to know an awful lot for a guard."

He turned and stared at me with those piercing green eyes. He reminded me of the way Léon had gazed at me earlier. A look that said he knows so much but couldn't say a word.

"Don't frown so much, you will give yourself wrinkles," he said mockingly, and carried on leading the way.

We took another sharp turn, climbed a flight of stairs and turned into a narrow hallway. We stopped at a door, went through it and ended up in a maintenance closet.

"Uh, where are we?"

"We are here."

"At the club?"

"Uh-huh."

Six

Sebastian opened the door, and we entered another hallway with dark blue walls and glow-in-the-dark stars. I felt like I was outside, surrounded by the Milky Way. The air in the hallway was crisp and cool. We walked to the end of the hallway, and Sebastian knocked on a door, then opened it without waiting for an answer.

Léon was sitting on a black leather sofa, or rather he was elegantly draped over it like he was waiting for someone to take his picture for GQ Magazine. I stifled my urge to giggle.

The sofa was facing a two-way mirror that looked out onto a bar, where the bartender served patrons and people dancing near the DJ stand.

"I'm glad you came," Léon said, but his expression was complex and straight-faced. I couldn't yet tell if he was happy, sad, excited, or angry. His face and body looked as if someone had carved him from stone. Again, there was that flicker of his eyes toward me, his mouth slightly parted like he wanted to say something but couldn't or wouldn't.

To say, *'thank's for inviting me'*, sounded lame, so instead I said, "Me too."

I smiled when he did.

"Is this just a dance club?" I asked as I watched the bar area and the people swarming around the bartender for a drink.

"It is a dance club among other things." He smirked. "It's managed by Roland, who is also the star of the show. If you stay long enough, you might see his performance."

"What kind of performance?"

Léon's lips curved upward, and his eyes held a splash of mystery.

"Make sure she stays for the show, Sebastian." He rose in one swift motion as if pulled by strings and closed the distance between us.

I stepped backward but stopped when I hit Sebastian's chest behind me. I was sure he was beside me when we entered. I hadn't seen him move.

Léon stared at the man behind me and added, "I asked Sebastian to bring you here to let you know my private investigator has a few leads and will get back to us soon."

"Thank you. Did he say when?"

"No, but give him a day or two," Léon said. His eyes darted to Sebastian behind me, and it wasn't a friendly stare.

Something swirled in the air like hot water against my skin. My hands became clammy, and something tightened in my chest. The two men crowded me, one so close behind that I had no escape and could easily rip my body apart with his were-leopard strength and the other who was capable of draining my blood with a single bite.

I wasn't magical, but I could feel this; beating on, against and through me.

With Sebastian being a were-leopard, their metaphysical

display meant that he was powerful. And Léon, Master Vampire of the City, had hundreds, if not thousands, of vampires and were-animals at his beck-and-call with which to feed into his power supply.

As I stood between them, their power slammed into me. I doubled over, gripped the edge of the sofa and sidestepped away. The air was cooler now that I was outside of their power circle. I inhaled slowly, exhaled and rubbed my hands together.

They continued staring at each other fiercely. If I didn't know better, it appeared as though they were talking mind-to-mind, and it wasn't a happy conversation.

Sebastian was a security guard for Léon, and he was disrespecting his master.

Léon bunched his fists, his pale hands appeared ghost-like.

I glanced from one to the other and said, "What's going on? You look like you want to kill each other."

Léon stared at me with those ocean-blue eyes that I so frequently became lost in. There was a blank expression across his face that I didn't understand.

I turned to Sebastian, whose usual grass-green eyes were bleeding to the color of sea-weed.

"It doesn't concern you," Sebastian said.

"Are you sure?" Léon asked, cocking his head to the side.

Sebastian remained defiant, his eyes locked upon his master.

After a moment, Léon conceded, "Must be my mistake. Then, no, it doesn't concern you." His eyes flitted to me again.

"I can leave." I said, pointing to the two-way mirror through which I could see the club attendees having fun. Maybe it was time for me to join them. I didn't know what was going on with these two, but I had enough of my own problems.

When neither responded, I headed for the door. With no idea

how to find the entrance to the dance floor, I was ready to try every single door until I found a way.

Léon spoke rapidly in French, and Sebastian answered him in French. Whatever was said, it didn't sound pleasant.

Sebastian left the other man and caught up with me. Once in the hallway, I wasn't sure which way to turn, so I stopped and allowed him to pass. He darted toward another closed door, and once through it, I found myself in a storeroom filled with liquor and faced with another door which lead out to the actual bar area.

As we entered the club, hot air hit me in the face and I wondered how the patrons danced in this heat. There were four beautiful ladies dancing in cages that hung from the ceilings. They had strips of leather wrapped around their bodies covering their modesty. They flashed fangs and danced provocatively in their cages.

Sebastian nodded at the bartender, who gave a slight nod in return and carried on tending to his thirsty patrons.

"Would you like something to drink?"

"I don't know what I like," I said, which sounded pitiful to me.

"Cocktails are a good start. Wait here." He went into the bar area and started mixing like he worked there. People tried to get his attention, but he ignored them.

Near the bar was a blonde woman held by a tall man. She tilted her head to one side while he pushed her long auburn hair out of his way. He kissed her neck gently; once, then twice, before opening his mouth to bite. One hand gripped her shoulder whilst the other was wrapped around her waist. She lay loose-limbed in his arms, like a rag doll. Her head fell backward in pleasure as the vampire fed on her. He stopped, looked at me and smiled, flecks of blood on his lips. He touched his lips and sucked hard on his finger; he was clearly an exhibitionist. I turned my attention elsewhere.

Near the dance floor, a man in tight leather pants and naked from the waist up danced in front of a redhead. They shared a few laughs, and he nodded and offered her his neck. She wrapped her arms around his broad shoulders and fed, his eyes fluttering and his mouth parted. He cupped her ass with both hands, and before she stopped, he pushed his groin into hers and held it there until he opened his eyes again. He almost collapsed, but she held onto him until he could walk unaided.

All these humans were more than willing to offer their necks —their blood—for that slice of vampiric heaven.

Sebastian returned with two martini glasses filled with pink liquid.

"What is it?"

He handed one to me. "Take a sip."

I sipped the cool liquid, finding it sweet and strong. It definitely contained more than one shot of alcohol.

"It's good."

"Come, let's go to our table."

He led us away from the bar area. As we navigated through the throng of people, I didn't see either of the couples that I had watched again. We climbed the stairs against the side of the warehouse to the first floor. There were soft sofas, bar stools and a few VIP tables with bouncers guarding a tiny rope that hung on poles that came up to our knees.

Sebastian shook hands with a large African male who looked like he could put you in a coma with one flat-handed slap. He said something to Sebastian, and they both turned to look at me. I glanced around, conscious that they were talking about me. I chose that moment to take another sip of the sweet slush and enjoyed the cool liquid as it went down my throat.

Both men smiled, and Sebastian motioned for me to walk with him to the top area. As we approached, I saw that the space was occupied by numerous people that I had never seen before. Sebastian leaned in close with his mouth near to my ear to make himself heard over the loud music.

"Some are vampires, and some are food; just don't give into any of their bullshit. And, just remember they are just messing with you. Don't take them too seriously."

Great. I might not remember a lot, but I knew that vampires could be tricky bastards who would mind-fuck you till Sunday and make you come back for more. I so did not want to mingle with nasty vamps tonight.

"Just as long as they don't think I'm food."

Sebastian didn't hear. I touched his shoulder; he stopped and bent his head so that it was close to mine. I went onto my tiptoes, and being near his neck, I could smell the ocean and the scent of citrus mixed with a hint of leaves and grass. And underneath each of those smells was *him*. My hand held onto his one arm, and I felt his muscles flex as I repeated what I had said, close to his ear.

He laughed. "Don't worry, they know," he said, winking wickedly.

Sebastian put his hand on the small of my back and started introducing me to everyone as '*the girl from the alley*' because that's where they had found me, and they didn't know what to call me since I couldn't remember my name.

I heard someone say, '*Her name is Alley?*'

I rolled my eyes at him, but it was funny and I laughed. I guess Alley wasn't too far off, and I didn't know what my name actually was, so I could be Alley for now.

The first person Sebastian introduced me to was Jean-René, a vampire with his apéritif—a woman in her early twenties—

nestled closely to his side. Jean-René had pale skin and ice-blue colored eyes, wavy brown hair in need of a trim that curled around his face, and he had a week's worth of stubble. He had a pretty face, but he didn't look female. He was of average build, similar to that of a swimmer, and he was tall even when seated.

I remembered that when a person turned into a vampire, they would remain how they had looked on their last day of mortality. Despite most vampires having a tendency for meticulousness, I didn't think that he had shaved much when he was human.

Jean-René introduced his 'date' as Candy, who looked very similar to a lot of other blonde girls with blue eyes who starved themselves to stay skinny.

Next to Candy was Charlotte, another vampire with porcelain-like skin and flaming red hair that danced around her shoulders as she spoke and when she laughed. She had crystal green eyes with a dark green circle around her iris, and pouty ruby lips. She wore a skintight red dress that didn't leave much to the imagination. The man beside her, Mark, glanced at me with large, imploring eyes, pursed lips and a bleeding neck.

Next to Mark was more 'food'. Her skin a chocolate-brown color, a shaved head and long eyelashes. She was comforting Mark by holding his left hand. She smiled at me, and I smiled back. I didn't hear her name as there was a change in DJ's and the new one put music on with harder, much louder beats. I got Ian's name; he was the vampire who had his right arm draped over his date. Ian was beautiful in every sense. He had hypnotic blue eyes—the lightest of blues with a ring of darkest blue around the iris—and short, straight black hair. He had a square jaw, full lips, and the straightest nose I'd ever seen.

But, even with all his beauty, there was something vaguely sinister in the way he held onto his 'food', with an intensely possessive glint in his eyes. I couldn't put my finger on it, but he exuded a certain perilousness that I never wanted to experience.

Lastly, there was Esther. She had hazel-colored eyes, long brown hair, and a beauty mark on her right cheek near her top lip. Her *'food'* looked like he was related to the Ian's date; he too had a shaved head and long eyelashes, and seemed very comfortable sitting with the predators. His name was Declan.

I gave a smile that twitched at the ends, said, 'Hi,' to everyone and gulped down some cocktail. The half-moon-shaped sofa that the four couples were sitting on also had enough space for Sebastian and I. We sat at the far end, consciously leaving enough space between them and us, and I removed my jacket and draped it over the high-back of the sofa. The sofa reminded me of a space-aged booth from a nineties TV show. I remembered all these weird odd's and end's, yet I still couldn't remember my name, who I was, or what I was doing in that alley.

The music was deafening, and I couldn't hear the vampires or their *'food'* speak, so I watched the people on the dance floor below us. There were women adorned with neck wounds, who had lost their shirts revealing their bras.

Others were drenched in sweat and carried on drinking and dancing like their lives depended on it. There were a few holding onto their partners, offering their necks, and the vampires bit down and drank from them, just enough to quench their thirsts.

I didn't notice anyone fainting or being carried out. One thing was clear: *everyone* was having a good time. At some *'humans only'* bars, they would drink until they were drunk, and that's when the fights would break out. Not here; everyone enjoyed themselves.

I stared at some of the humans, those with bite marks. They

wandered aimlessly around the dance floor area or had their arms hooked around their vampire partner's waist, the vampire keeping them upright. They looked positively delirious.

There was another change in the music and then it stopped. The silence echoed in my ears as the room darkened. A beam of light shone on one person who stood in the centre of the dance area. I hadn't seen the people move out of the way, and then they surrounded him in a crescent.

The man had long brown hair which hung to his shoulders and wore a suit that moulded to his body, revealing broad shoulders and a slim, muscled waist beneath. I couldn't see the color of his eyes, but they looked dark and were framed by sharp features; a straight nose, high cheekbones, strong jaw. As he spoke, shadows played along his cheekbones.

I watched him, keeping my eyes on his face and the way his lips moved as he spoke. His words slithered down the length of my spine and down to my toes, and all the hairs on my body stood on end. I couldn't comprehend what those words were, but they made me quiver in my seat.

I tore my eyes away from him and at the crowd instead, and it wasn't just me it was happening to. Everyone, men and women alike, stared at him. We were all spellbound, waiting for his pleasure to caress us.

The only words I heard were; *'desire'*, *'delight'*, *'enjoyment'* and *'who wants a kiss?'* All the women near him raised their hands. He walked through the sea of ladies searching for volunteers; some touched his shoulders, others ran their fingers over and down his back, while two tried to unsuccessfully wrap their bodies around his, his arm brushing them aside.

He selected two women and brought them back to where he had first started. The brunette stood on his left, her mouth opened in a surprised *'O'*. He closed the distance between them, cupped her face between his hands and drew her in for a kiss. It was a chaste kiss at first. He pulled away to glance at her, and then at the crowd. He smiled before kissing her again. This time, it was hard and passionate as he explored the inside of her mouth. She wrapped her arms around him so tightly that I couldn't see where he ended and she began. When the kiss ended, her body went limp in his arms. Security assisted the vampire and carried her to the sofa against the wall. Her eyes were closed, and her face slack.

The other woman, a redhead, stared wide-eyed at everyone with her arms crossed over her chest. Her eyes darted from the brunette on the sofa to the crowd and then to the vampire before her. With an index finger, the vampire touched her shoulder, and her arms dropped to her sides. He held both her arms, brought her closer to him until she was pressed firmly against his chest, and he kissed her; again, it was chaste, then aggressive, but still this side of enjoyable. Watching that kiss made things tighten down below, and heat crept up my neck and face.

The vampire let go of the redhead, blood dripping down his chin. He wiped the blood off with a white handkerchief that he pulled from his chest pocket. The redhead licked her bleeding lip, then her knees buckled, and security caught her before she fell to the floor. They sat her next to the brunette to allow them both to recover.

The crowd fell silent, my pulse raced in my ears, and then the crowd started clapping. I heard gasps of 'Oh, My God!' and a cascade of giggling.

Someone touched my shoulder, and I flinched. It was Sebastian. The smile on his face suggested he knew exactly what I had experienced along with every other women in the dance club, and asked if I was all right? I held my hand in front of my mouth as I giggled and nodded. I didn't trust my voice at that moment.

He continued staring at me with amusement in his eyes.

After a moment I could finally speak and said, "What's the name of this club again?"

"*Kiss*," he said.

I swallowed hard and felt my eyes widen. *Kiss*. Shit. I had found a ticket stub from this club in the car. I'd been here before the attack. I wished I had checked the date on the ticket. A knot formed in the pit of my stomach. I downed the rest of my drink but kept the empty glass in my hands as I watched the rest of the people downstairs. I tried to think of other things; tried to get my mind off the car and the discovery of the torso, if only for a moment.

I watched the vampire move through the crowd; he spoke to a few women while others tried to get a piece of what the two women had just experienced. He was a walking chick magnet. The men—the humans—had to be jealous. He must be Roland, the star of the show Léon had mentioned earlier in his office. I shivered, but it wasn't from being cold.

Before I could think of anything else, Sebastian came in front of me again and asked if I wanted another drink. I nodded, glancing at everyone sitting near us, I didn't want to be left alone with them. I rose when he did and grabbed his hand; he squeezed my hand in his.

I stood on the side of the bar with the rest of the patrons while Sebastian poured another round. I had my back to the DJ stand, but when a song that I liked came on, I danced where I stood and turned around to face the gyrating people all around. Someone came from the right and grabbed my hand and pulled me toward all the bodies on the dance floor. I didn't know who was pulling on my hand, but he held it tightly. He was large, at least six foot four, and wore a black fishnet shirt with tight leather pants.

"Let go," yelled, but he didn't hear. Nobody heard me over the loud music.

I glanced back at the bar, but there were so many people surrounding me I couldn't see Sebastian anymore. I tugged my hand back harder, but the man was strong, and he wasn't relenting.

Hair rose on the back of my neck. My pulse thundered in my ears. My only thought was to get away from him. If this stranger got me out of the club and no one saw me, I would be gone for good.

A glance at his hip revealed a gun underneath his fishnet shirt, and I pulled harder. There were 'No guns' signs plastered all around the club, yet he was able to keep his.

The man got me all the way to the other side of the club near to the 'Exit' sign and pulled me into his arms before he let go of my hand. With the movement of his pull, I fell against his chest but kept both my hands in front of me, so that my hands were pinned against his chest, providing some distance between us. He wrapped his arms around me and leaned in as if he wanted a kiss.

I leaned as far back as I could. The more I struggled, the tighter he squeezed me, and my chest started to ache. Finally, I stopped struggling, and his mouth came close to my ear.

"Relax, I'm not trying to hurt you. You don't remember me?" he asked.

"No," I said, yelling into his ear.

"I'm sorry for grabbing you like that, but I had to get you away from him. When I saw you standing alone, I had to take the chance. I'm on your side."

He pulled a card from a pocket in the front of his pants and held it up so I could see. It was a card with only a number on it.

"My name is Ralph. Hide this, and call me if you need me, day or night. You can't trust any of them. Not the vampire, not the were-leopard—*none* of them. To prove you can trust me, ask them about their connection to each other."

He pulled away and regarded me. He had dark blue eyes, full lips, a beard and wavy dark brown hair that touched his shoulders. He had broad shoulders and a defined pectoral triangle; he was all muscle.

Slowly, Ralph started to loosen his grip and leaned in again. "Don't believe what they tell you." He let go of me and pushed through the crowd until he reached the 'Exit' door and left.

I stood with my arms bunched up close to my chest. I tucked the card in my hand into the little pocket on the side of my satin skirt as a hand touched my shoulder. I flinched, spun around and hit the person who touched me. Cocktail glasses went crashing to the floor, and Sebastian stared down at me like I had sprouted a second head.

The music was so loud that nobody heard the glasses shatter on the floor.

Sebastian kept his distance, held his hands up and yelled over the beats, "I didn't know you could fight."

The surprised look on my face must have shown because I didn't know either. I put my feet together and stood straight. "I'm sorry I hit you. You gave me a fright."

"Who was that? One moment I was making us drinks, the next some man was pulling you away."

So, Sebastian *had* seen the mysterious Ralph. Given what Ralph had said to me, I wondered if him being noticed would mean anything to my 'protector', but if it did, I couldn't tell from Sebastian's manner.

I decided to downplay my interaction with Ralph. "I don't know," I said. "I told him to leave me alone, and he did."

"Are you all right?"

"Uh-huh." I nodded quickly and rubbed my hands together. They were stinging after hitting Sebastian.

"Come, let's get more drinks."

I stayed with Sebastian in the bar area while he made another round of cocktails. He gave me mine, offered me his hand, and we walked back up to the VIP area. There were more people upstairs now than before, sitting at the other tables, but our seats were still available.

Ian's *'food'* had lost her shirt, and her head was against the sofa as he embraced her. He was drinking from her slender neck, and as we approached them, he glared at me. The thought behind those eyes told me he wanted to do awful things to her. I heard her moan as her eyes rolled back into her head. I felt my mouth part as I watched.

It was only when Sebastian spoke to me that I closed my mouth.

"Cherry seems to enjoy it," Sebastian said as we sat down.

So that's her name; *Cherry.*

Candy was straddling Jean-René's lap. He was kissing her so hard I thought he would come out of the other side of her. She had her hands in his hair while his cupped her ass.

Charlotte was sitting in Mark's lap, mimicking Jean-René and Candy as though they were competing for *'Who wore it better?'.*

Esther stared longingly at Sebastian. I gaped at him as he took a long, drawn-out sip from his cocktail and watched Jean-René and Candy. Either he was ignoring Esther, or he had no clue how she felt about him.

Declan seemed asleep against Esther's shoulder. When she

rose, Declan slumped over and fell onto Cherry's lap. Cherry was completely in Ian's grasp and didn't seem to notice the man now lying on her.

Ian stopped feeding, and Cherry's head lolled to one side and fell on top of Declan's back. *Shit.* I couldn't see their chests rise and fall. I wanted to ask Sebastian if they were dead, but Esther pushed my drink to my lips and mouthed the word, *"Drink."* She approached Sebastian and opened her legs on either side of his and waited for him to notice her. The music quietened a little, and I could hear the vampires on the couch. I took a long sip from my drink while I watched Sebastian's face as he registered that Esther was standing near him.

"Don't you miss me, Seb?" Esther touched his hair.

Sebastian grabbed her hand and moved it away.

Seb. That was the first time I had heard anybody shorten his name. I downed my drink and placed the empty glass on the floor before the fireworks started next to me.

Esther fell forward and grabbed Sebastian's shoulders, her face painfully close to his. He leaned backward until his back hit the cushion, but Esther was persistent. She knelt on the couch beside Sebastian, her complete attention fixated on him.

"What are you doing, Esther?"

"I miss you, Seb," she said, her lips lightly brushing his as she spoke.

He moved his face away from hers so that they weren't touching, grabbed her wrists and pushed her away from him.

Undeterred, Esther straddled him and held onto his neck. She leaned into me and said, "We used to share a bed." She winked and smiled sinisterly.

Before she could utter anything else, Sebastian stood with her attached to his lap. She wrapped her legs tighter around his waist as he walked with her to the other side of the couch and pushed her onto it.

I felt movement beside me. As I turned, Ian pressed his lips against mine. He was gentle at first, his warm mouth against mine, then he tried to open my mouth with his tongue. Ian held one hand against the back of my head to stop me from pulling away and the other around my throat.

I froze. I didn't want him kissing me, and I didn't want to be a victim. I pushed against his chest but he was stronger; he had powers I couldn't fathom. But I still pushed as hard as I could. The more I resisted, the harder he forced himself against me until his tongue was inside my mouth. His kiss was hard and desperate. When his tongue came between my teeth, I bit down with every bit of strength I had. A metallic-tasting liquid filled our mouths, and I swallowed it. He pulled away, laughing, as blood trickled from his mouth.

The kiss sent shivers down my spine and through my body. It was now clear to me that the hunger in Ian's blue eyes wasn't for food, but for lascivious desires.

"You taste wonderful." He touched his bottom lip with his finger and licked the blood slowly. "Can I bite you back?" Ian closed the gap between us, leaned closer, and opened his mouth, flashing fangs.

Everything seemed to happen at once. He was closing in on my neck when my elbow caught his jaw. With his forward momentum, I lifted my arms, pushing him away from me, and he fell off the sofa.

The other vampires stared at us.

Ian stood quickly, like someone had pulled on his strings, and flew into me. We crashed to the floor, his long body pinning mine. He pushed my legs apart enough for his own to slide between mine. The more I struggled, the harder he pressed against me, and I could feel how happy he was to be there. I pulled on my arms but he held my wrists above my head, leaned in and kissed my cheek gently.

"You smell wonderful," he said as he breathed in my scent and nuzzled my neck.

"Get off me," I said, my voice strained.

My pulse thundered in my ears, and my breathing became labored as Ian pushed harder against me. The ceiling above us swirled.

"But I've only just started playing with you," he said, laughing. He rubbed his nose against my cheek and brushed his lips against mine. "Hmm, you taste so good. Just one bite, please," he implored, whispering.

Ian lowered one hand to cup my face, to force me to look at him, then moved my head away to bare my neck. He opened his mouth and hissed, his fangs edging closer to my neck. Out of the corner of my eye, I saw someone quickly move, and that someone pulled Ian off me. Ian flew across the VIP area and crashed into the mirror against the far wall. Sebastian towered above me, proffered his hand, and pulled me to my feet.

"Come, I think it's time we left. Ian gets pissy when things don't go his way, and I doubt you want to open a vein for him?"

I took Sebastian's hand and stood closer to him.

The other vampires rose, edging nearer, leering at us.

We ran down the stairs before Ian could stand up and fight.

Seven

"I'm sorry about what happened back there with the vampires. Esther and Ian are usually much more controlled than that."

I gave Sebastian the look that the vampires deserved, but because he was near instead, he got it.

"I shouldn't have taken you there. I'm sorry. Did he hurt you?"

"Not much." My side ached more than before, but I would live. "What was that, Sebastian?"

"They're vampires. It's what they do. They were testing you, sorry." A pained expression crossed his pleasant face.

It wasn't his fault, and he had helped me to get out of there, but why were they testing me in the first place? All I knew was that we had got out and nobody had died, although I couldn't be entirely sure about the vampires' *'food'*.

We ran back to the warehouse. I honestly couldn't describe it in any other way. It's a warehouse made into a maze by its moving walls, which served its purpose of confusing the bad guy or good gal.

I trailed behind Sebastian with my hand still in his. His palm felt so warm. I'd only known him for a few days, during what could possibly be the worst days of my life, but somewhere deep inside, there was something. Whatever that something was, I didn't know if it meant I could trust him.

The scruffy-looking man in the fishnet shirt from the club had told me I couldn't trust Léon or Sebastian, but could I trust *him*? I didn't know who Ralph was or how he knew me.

My head started to ache thinking about it all, and I was no closer to discovering who I was or what I'd been doing in that alley.

When we arrived at Léon's room, I had a full-blown headache and my mouth was dry. Sebastian pushed the door open, and we saw a naked woman sitting on someone with the silk sheets spilling around her body. She turned to us but didn't cover herself.

Léon peered around the naked woman's body and smiled. "That was quick, Sebastian. I see that you two are already holding hands?"

I didn't know if he or I was embarrassed, but we let go of each other's hand at the exact same time.

"Don't stop on my account," Léon said through heavy breaths. He gripped the woman's hips and started thrusting inside her. She arched backward as she screamed in pleasure. After she spasmed around him, Léon pushed her to one side, and she huddled in the sheets to bask in the afterglow. Léon climbed out of the bed and walked to us. I didn't want to look anywhere except for his forehead.

"I hope you don't mind, my dear, but I will be here for the

rest of the evening." Léon had a grin splashed across his face as he stood in front of me.

I stared at the fine lines of his forehead. "It's your place."

"Sebastian, you don't mind, do you?" Léon asked.

The men leered at each other, their powers flaring up to the point that they felt almost tangible, like tiny insects biting across my skin. I gasped and stepped back until I knocked my head against the door frame.

"Best you take her now before she hurts herself." Léon turned toward the bathroom.

"Come, let's go," Sebastian said, taking my hand.

"What's up with him?"

"He gets like that sometimes. Just ignore it."

We walked to Sebastian's room, which was only three doors down and was identical to Léon's. The only difference between the two was that Sebastian's bathroom was smaller. When I entered the room from the bathroom, Sebastian was heading out the door.

"Where are you going?"

"You stay here, and I will bunk with one of the other leopards."

"Don't be silly. You've slept beside me before when you healed me. It will be fine. We're only sleeping next to each other." What I didn't say was that I might have a husband and a child somewhere and a casual anything isn't what I needed right now. But that didn't mean I wanted to be alone, either.

"I don't mind if you don't?" he said.

"No, I don't mind."

I wanted to ask if Léon was always such an ass, but then I remembered the other vampires at the club.

Sebastian sat on a chair with his back to me and removed his shoes. His shirt strained against his back, and it reminded me of

Ralph. He had said that I should ask Sebastian about his connection with Léon.

"Can I ask you something?"

"Sure."

"What kind of relationship do you and Léon have?"

"Why do you ask?" The lines between his eyes deepened, and his gaze intensified.

I didn't think that I could get away with feigning curiosity, but the alternative was admitting that Ralph had suggested it to me, and that he had warned me against trusting them. There was no way I was ready to tell Sebastian that.

"The two of you seem to fight often? What is it with the two of you, or is that just the relationship you have with your master?"

His body stiffened, and he gave a long sigh. "He is not *my* master. He is *the* master of the city. There is a difference."

I crossed my arms and leaned against the bedpost. "What does that mean?"

His shoes fell to the floor, and he threw his socks into the laundry basket. He stood, a full head and shoulders taller than me at about six-foot-two. As he stepped closer, dark shadows played along his face, accentuating his high cheekbones. He closed the gap between us while I stepped away from the bed—away from him—until I reached the wall near the door. I didn't know why I did that; he had done nothing except help me, yet in that moment I knew I had to move away.

When he realized I was moving closer to the door, he stopped and lifted his hands to indicate he meant no harm. He sat on the bed and untucked his shirt.

"I'm sorry. I didn't mean to scare you. You don't have to run for the door." He sighed.

"I'm just cautious, I guess. I mean, I don't know you. Or

Léon, for that matter. You welcomed me into your home, but I'm scared. I guess Ian attacking me earlier shook me up." I stepped closer to him. "And the power unleashed between the two of you burns my skin and makes it hard for me to breathe around you both."

His brows furrowed. "What do you mean? You can feel our power?"

"Yes."

His confusion was evident. "You are human; you shouldn't feel anything."

Shit.

"What do you mean—can't everyone feel power?" I frowned. Why didn't I know this? I knew enough information about vampires and were-animals, but I clearly knew little about their powers.

"No, a human shouldn't be able to pick up on any meta-physical power, unless they themselves have some kind of ability."

"But I don't have any ability. Or, at least, not one I remember having," I said, frustration burning inside me. "Your powers set me off so badly I can't breathe and my skin burns, but I don't know why I can feel them."

He considered that for a moment. "That's interesting."

I was hoping he would share a little more, but one thing I knew about Sebastian was that he wasn't one for words. I allowed him a moment to think before returning to the subject of Léon.

"Come on, what's the deal with the two of you? You are always fighting—like siblings." I narrowed my eyes.

"It's a long story."

I pressed on. "I don't have any other plans. And we have all night."

Sebastian remained hesitant, but eventually his shoulders sagged, and he gave in. "We are related."

"Related how?"

"We're brothers."

I choked back a laugh. "Are you serious?"

The look he gave me told me that he was.

"As in *real* brothers?"

He nodded.

"But he is a vampire and you are a were-leopard? How does something like that happen?"

"It's rare," he admitted.

I sat beside him on the bed and whispered, "Are you really blood brothers?"

He smiled, almost laughing. "*Blood brothers.* That's funny. We have the same father but different mothers. Our father became a vampire when he was twenty-eight and was still able to procreate. Léon was born a vampire and tore through his human mother's womb, killing her. Two years later, I was born to a were-leopard."

My mouth gaped open for a heartbeat. I thought that I had heard it all, but this was beyond me. "But Léon is eight-hundred years old, and you just said that you are twenty-eight. I don't understand how that can be? And I thought vampires were created, not born."

"When humans turn into vampires, some can still have babies with humans or were-animals in human form. Apparently, it's rare for the babies to survive. After our father became a vampire, he had us. He became a legend within the vampire community, so to speak. Léon was born a vampire and didn't have to be bitten. He grew up like a normal child, only instead of it taking twenty-eight years, he reached adulthood within five. Two years after Léon was born, our father fell in love with a were-leopard, and they conceived a child. Nine months later, I was born. I aged quickly during the first five years until I was twenty-eight, and I have appeared that age ever since."

"You are also around eight-hundred years old?"

"Yes."

"I still don't understand how that can be. The literature I remember said that were-animals aged slowly, but you aren't aging at all."

"We think I have some of our father's traits."

"But why do you hide?"

"You mean, why do I work as Léon's guard?"

I nodded.

"Practicality. Despite how things may appear, we've always been close. When he became Master of the City, he needed me and the were-animals to forge an alliance, and it made sense for me to be by his side. Together we are stronger; we are more powerful."

"So, people know you are related?"

"Some do, I'm sure." He shrugged. "It's not a secret."

"People could use that against you, or more likely, against Léon. Aren't you worried about that? Or about me? I could be one of those people sent to kill you."

"I don't see you as a threat. Well—not yet." He flashed a wide smile.

His attempt at humor failed. I wasn't happy. I stared at him.

"You are way too serious now."

"And you aren't serious enough, Sebastian. What if I hadn't forgotten who I am? What if me being here means that you're in danger?" I said, raising my voice, with my pulse raging in my ears.

Power trickled off him until it seemed to fill the room. It

swirled around me, through me, so that the tense muscles in my back and shoulders relaxed and I suddenly felt tired.

I frowned at him. "What was that?"

"You needed to calm down. You are a very angry person." He pointed two fingers toward my heart. "There is something inside of you so similar to that of a glowing-red poking iron that it can scald everybody around you."

"What does that mean?" I sounded angry, even in spite of my tiredness.

He didn't answer, and the silence was deafening. He gave me cold green eyes like ice over a lake.

My shoulders rounded and slumped forward. "Okay, all right. Stop whatever you are doing. I need to sleep." My adrenaline rush was receding; it had kept me alive during the fight with the vampires at the club and had helped me to cope with the man who grabbed my hand. And now, the power flare up from Sebastian had knocked the anger and stubbornness right out of me, and all I felt was exhaustion.

I glanced around his room. My eyes scanned the cupboard where he kept his clothes, the two chairs near the table in the middle of the room and the large bed made from elegantly carved, vintage wood that I was sitting on, its four posts reaching the ceiling.

"Why are there no clocks in any of the rooms? I keep having to ask you for the time." I folded my arms across my chest, and as my right arm went under my left arm, I felt that I was missing something important. Something that I kept close to my heart.

I gasped. "I was wearing a shoulder holster. I was wearing a gun that evening. When I saw Elena with her holster, it didn't register. I didn't remember, not until now."

"There was no gun on you when we brought you in, and your holster had to be cut away."

"Was there a phone?"

His face thawed, the ice in his eyes melting as his mouth pressed into a straight line. He shook his head gently and said, "No, there wasn't a phone either. It was just the key chain we found in the alley that we thought might be yours. There was nothing else on your person when we found you. Nothing."

I wiped tears from my eyes, and my breath shook.

"We went through your car carefully and we found nothing of value and no personal belongings."

"And, the man in the trunk?"

"So far, he is a torso and a severed hand, and that's all. We still don't know who he was, but Kit is looking into it."

"Did you say, 'severed hand'? I didn't see one."

"We found it after we removed everything from the trunk. Kit is using the hand to take fingerprints."

"Did you pass this on to the police?"

"No, they are… otherwise indisposed with other crimes, and this—even though there's a victim—isn't important enough. There are just too many politicians running the force at the moment." Either his voice was tinged with sadness, or he was tired.

The details were a little vague, but I started to remember something about a vampire trying to run for governor and wanted to cut funding at police stations. The humans and vampires were in a political battle of sorts. It was all interesting to remember, but it was a problem for another time.

I kicked my shoes off and climbed under the silk green sheets wearing my clothes, I was too tired to do anything else.

Sebastian removed his clothing down to his boxers, pulled on a soft sleep t-shirt and climbed in beside me. He switched off the light on his side, and we both lay on our backs in the dark.

I had an urgent need to be held, and didn't want to sound

silly by asking him. I did anyway. "Would you mind if I snuggled against you until I fall asleep?"

He moved to the middle of the bed and whispered, "Sure."

I came in closer and he opened his arm for me so that I could nestle my head between his shoulder and chest and he held me.

It didn't take long to fall asleep in his warm arms, listening to the strong beat of his heart.

Eight

I stood in front of a mirror with a tall green tree behind me. Léon was lying on the bed with crimson silk sheets spilled around him, covering him from the waist down. He held his hand out for me.

"No."

"Why not?"

"No," I repeated. I didn't want to go to him.

"Is this better?" He stood behind me dressed in a white dress shirt with gold cuff links and a golden tie. His dark hair hung in his face, and as he swept it aside, his blue eyes caressed my body as he watched me in the mirror.

I spun around to face him. "Why are you in my dream, Léon?"

"I wanted to see if it was possible."

"Okay, now you have, you can go. You said you wanted nothing from me. Have you changed your mind?"

"No," he said.

I blinked, and suddenly I was sitting on warm sand under an

umbrella, basking in the sunlight. I was in a one-piece bathing suite with a cocktail in my hand, the same mix as Sebastian had made at the club. As I took a sip, I saw Sebastian emerge from the cerulean sea. His blonde hair darker, water glistened off his toned body, his swim trunks fitting loosely around his hips. When he reached me, he bent down and picked up a towel, starting to dry the water off his body. The water shimmered as it dripped down his abdomen, and I wanted to lick it off. Still not completely dry, he lay the towel down beside me and sat on it.

"It's beautiful, isn't it?" he said, staring out onto the water.

"Why are you in my dream?" I asked, frowning at him.

"I wanted to see if it was possible."

He sounded just like Léon. He leaned closer to whisper in my ear, and as he did so, his left hand came near to my face. Only it wasn't his hand—it was claws surrounded by black fur.

I awoke alone and in Sebastian's room. My clothing was damp and my breathing strained. I laid back down on the bed and rubbed the sides of my head with my middle fingers. Tears rolled down the sides of my face and ran into my ears.

The tree was gone; there was no mirror, no beach and no claws. I exhaled and sat up, seeing a clock on the other side of the bed that hadn't been there last night. It was already after four in the afternoon. Another day I'd slept through. It was time to get up.

I climbed out of bed and ran a hot bath. The smell of trees after a storm, tall grass from wild fields and the smell of fog above moving water. The coarse fur brushed against my cheek but I couldn't see it; I could only feel it.

My eyes fluttered open at the sight of the familiar tiles in Sebastian's bathroom. It must've been flashbacks I was remembering from the attack. The were-animal that hurt me; the smell of it, the feel of it. I remembered black fur or it was dark charcoal in color. Then I smelled the ocean with a hint of citrus, but that was Sebastian's scent that I was smelling.

I sank into the water until my whole body was submerged. When I surfaced I saw the soap was in the shower, along with the shampoo and conditioner; I had forgotten to fetch it before I climbed into the bath. But I didn't feel like getting out. The towels were also on the other side of the bathroom.

Shit. I wasn't thinking clearly. I couldn't remember whether I had locked the bathroom door either. The dream must have affected me more than I thought. And did I dream of Léon and Sebastian, or had they really entered my dream themselves?

There was a soft knock on the door.

"Who is it?"

"Sebastian. Can I come in?"

"Hold on."

The bath was as full as it would get without spilling over the sides. How much would he see? I lifted my legs and sat up, huddled my arms around my legs until I was sure nothing could be seen and said, "Okay, you can come in now."

He came in holding two mugs, the aroma of coffee trailing behind him.

"Hmm, that smells good."

He placed the cup on the edge of the bath, close enough for me to reach, and stood back.

"Thanks," I said. "How long have you been awake? I see it's already late afternoon."

"I've been up for a while. You needed rest, so I left you to sleep."

"How did you know I was awake to bring me coffee?"

"Léon told me."

"Doesn't he need to sleep in his coffin?"

Sebastian's laugh was deep, with a hint of a growl. "No; he's

83

a master vampire, he need not stay in his coffin all day like the rest of them. He usually gets up around four. I was already in the kitchen when he told me you were awake and might need company."

"Oh," I said, holding the mug with both hands, savoring each sip. I was slowly waking up and beginning to feel as normal as possible.

Sebastian placed his mug on the basin and went to the shower to pick up the soap, shampoo and conditioner. He set them on the edge of the bath. "It's only me who stays in this room and I prefer to shower. I don't have extra goodies for the bath."

They were the same French products that Léon used.

"What about Esther? Doesn't she share your room with you?" I cringed as the words flew from my mouth. By the time they were out, I couldn't take them back. It was none of my business.

"No, Esther was a one-time thing which I regret. She is crazy. Her old master ruined her and now she takes her crazy out on everyone."

"Sorry, I shouldn't have asked. It's none of my business. But, from what I saw last night, she seems to think otherwise."

"Like I said, she's crazy." He took a sip of his coffee. "Anyway, let me leave so you can finish. I'll come back in about thirty minutes to take you to the kitchen. I am sure you must be hungry by now."

"Ah yes, the moving walls. Are you scared I might go somewhere I'm not supposed to?" I snorted, putting my hand in front of my mouth in case there was another. I thought it was funny, but he did not. He left and closed the door behind him.

I washed my hair, and while the conditioner was doing what it was supposed to do, I washed my body. When I stood up, I could see the reflection of my body in the mirror on the opposite wall. I slowly pulled the large plaster from my side, revealing a pink raised scar that ran from my belly button all the way around my side to my spine. The stitches were the dissolvable kind, but there were some that still stuck out, and so I pulled them out. There were tiny scars that broke away from the larger one, where the bite marks tore through my body. It looked like a road map running across my abdomen. After only three days, it looked like a month's worth of healing. Impressive.

I finished bathing and wrapped a towel around my body and one around my hair. The bedroom was quiet. I had never noticed before, but the walls were probably thicker than normal because I couldn't hear anything from beyond Sebastian's or Léon's rooms; apart from the moving walls.

Standing between the bathroom's doorjamb, I realized I didn't have any clothes in Sebastian's room and sighed. As I moved closer to the bed, however, I saw that there was something on it; it was a stack of clothing with the key chain atop it and sneakers on the floor. I smiled.

Having dressed in jeans and a t-shirt, I slipped the card Ralph had given me and the key chain into the pockets of my jeans, one on either side. I towel-dried my hair and returned both towels to the bathroom.

When I entered the room again, Esther was sitting on the bed. My eyes flitted to the door, hoping someone would hear through the thick walls if Esther hurt me.

Esther was stunning in a pouty, porcelain doll kind of way. Her long brown hair was neatly brushed and stayed out of her face. The beauty spot on the right side of her face brought all attention to her full red lips and away from her hazel-colored eyes. She wore a tight pencil skirt and a low-cut blouse, revealing just a hint of cleavage.

"That was quite a show you put on last night. Ian doesn't like you much anymore." She curled a strand of hair between her thumb and index fingers.

"I don't enjoy being touched by someone I don't know."

Her shrill laughter made me flinch; it was so sudden and out of place. And loud.

"That's funny; you allow Sebastian to touch you."

"I don't allow anyone to touch me. Sebastian is only helping me."

She flew up from the bed in one sweeping motion and stood before me. Esther was a few inches taller than me, and as she leered down at me, her brown eyes bled to black with almost no white left. She flashed fangs as she laughed.

"Why are you so scared, human? I only want to talk."

"Standing so close to me and laughing like that isn't talking, Esther."

She raised her arms to attack, and I did two things at once. I blocked her right arm with my left, and because she was so close to me, I hit her on the side of her face and jaw area with my right elbow. She stepped back, stunned, and I kicked her in the solar plexus, knocking her backward onto the bed.

I ran to the door, but when I opened it, Ian was blocking my way. He saw Esther on the bed and me trying to escape, and grabbed my arms. He pinned my arms tightly behind my back and walked me backward until my head hit the far wall. He pushed me so hard that I bit my tongue; blood poured out from my mouth.

Ian pressed his body against mine, revealed fangs, and pressed his forehead against the side of my head. His breath hot against my cheek, he inched closer, licking the blood from my lips.

"I love it when a woman greets me with a mouth full of fresh blood." He turned to Esther and asked, "Are you all right, luv?"

"Kill her, she fucking hit me."

"It will be my pleasure."

I screamed as loud as I could, but it was too late. Ian opened his mouth, sinking his fangs into the curve of my neck. It hurt like nothing I had ever experienced. His bite turned acidic as his saliva mixed with my blood. He squeezed my arms tighter behind my back, and I started to shake. I tried moving my head a little, but as I did, his fangs tore my flesh as they sunk deeper into my neck.

I cried out again, and through shaky breaths, said, "Please let me go. It hurts."

Esther laughed again, her high-pitched cackling pierced my eardrums, and something wet dripped out from them and down the sides of my neck. She edged closer to Ian, draped an arm around him with her head on his shoulder and stared at me.

"Does it hurt, human?" Esther's tone hard and cold.

I didn't want to answer her. Tears filled my eyes, and I blinked them away; I would not cry in front of her.

Ian unlatched his jaw from my neck and licked the wound. It burned like hot coals against my skin.

He straightened his posture while still holding me tightly. "Her blood is divine, but she has a hint of something bitter, darker." He smacked his lips together, like one does when trying fine wine. "I think it's the best I've had from any human. You should try her, luv."

"No, no, no, no!" I cried, squeezing my eyes shut.

"Don't mind if I do. Ian, hold her tighter. I don't want her moving around."

Ian pulled my arms closer to one another behind my back. I cried out as my shoulders strained and he pushed his body firmly against mine, keeping me in place. "Hold her head, otherwise you can't get a good angle."

Esther held my face to one side and sank her fangs into the other side of my neck. She bit harder and faster, leaving me gasping for air. Ian's face blurred around the edges, a dense fog filled the room and the only thing keeping me up was Ian holding me against the wall. My body went limp against his, and pain shot from my neck down to the rest of me.

I heard the door fly open and hit the wall, and someone yelling in French. They didn't sound like friendly words. My eyes were too heavy to see, but I felt Esther release her fangs from my neck and Ian relaxing his grip from my arms as he stepped away.

With no one keeping me upright, I crumpled to the floor and fell into the darkness.

Nine

I waded through a lake rich and thick with blood. The tree standing on the embankment was as naked and lonely as I. The tree's bark was charred, and its leaves were burnt; it had been left to die. I swam toward the shore to reach it, but the more I swam, the further the tree was out of reach. When I stopped swimming, the crimson lake drained into the soil below and I was left standing with dried blood caked over my body.

Someone called out, but I couldn't make out the name. A name, no matter how hard I tried to remember, kept echoing farther and farther away until I couldn't hear it anymore. The calls stopped, and the silence rang in my ears.

"Do you like it?"

I spun around, and Léon stood before me, also caked in dried blood and with his fangs showing. I blinked. Sebastian stared back at me with bright green eyes and revealed his fangs. I blinked again and again until I could focus, but their faces transposed onto each other. Both men gazed at me, a mixture of blue, green, and gold slivers burning brightly in their eyes.

"It won't hurt," they said, biting into their wrists and offering their blood to me.

"No!" I yelled, shaking my head.

"You will die if you don't."

I squeezed my eyes shut. I didn't want what they were offering.

Silence.

My eyes fluttered open, and they were gone. The tree was gone. The dried blood was nowhere to be seen, and instead I wore a white slip dress, sitting in a white chair with a book in my hand with the title, *Ancient Egypt*.

I glanced at the open book, but the words shifted out of focus. Each word blended into another, and the pictures grayed out like a fog moving over water.

I rubbed my eyes and saw red smears on my hands. I stood, and the book dropped to the floor. I stepped over the book and walked toward the door, then everything blurred. Using the wall as my compass, I reached the open door, and my vision cleared. Sebastian stood holding his arms out to me, and I went to him.

"Help me," I said.

He held me to his chest, and the rhythm of his heartbeat eased my tension. One side of my face was against his clothing, but he moved, and then my face was against his naked skin. He held a knife, brought it closer to his chest and sliced into his skin above his nipple. Blood poured from the wound, and he held my face tightly to him until his blood reached my mouth.

"Drink, or you will die," he whispered. His tone serious.

I tried to push him away from me, but his blood poured into my mouth and down one side of my face. I swallowed the metallic liquid, and it burned down my throat. I coughed up the blood, but he kept pushing more and more of his life essence into my mouth.

I pushed harder against him, and finally he let go. I crashed to the ground and awoke with a jolt.

Arms held me down, and a male voice kept calmly saying, over and over, "Keep still, I won't hurt you."

The tension and anxiety I bottled up exploded inside my head and body, and I cried, "What is happening to me?"

Sebastian pulled me closer to him. Closer to his body, to the heat of his skin, and I held his body tightly against mine.

Ian and Esther had attacked me, draining me, almost killing me. I stiffened in Sebastian's arms.

"Léon pulled them off you in time. They are being punished for insubordination and what they did to you," he said.

"Punished how?" I asked, glancing into his face.

He stared down at me with a questionable expression. "What does it matter?" He shrugged, looking away. "It is a fate worse than death."

"Good. I want them to suffer." The words came out cold and cruel from my lips, but I didn't care.

The memory of their bites, their lips on my neck, and my blood loss prompted me to remember the dream; the crimson lake that had surrounded me.

I jumped out of Sebastian's arms and ran for the bathroom. I reached the toilet in time as I vomited rusty liquid. Once I was sure I had nothing more to puke, I shuddered and pulled the handle. I washed my face and stared in the mirror. I was in the same jeans and t-shirt I had pulled on before Ian and Esther attacked me. My skin was pale, my eyes were sunken and my cheeks were gaunt. I looked like shit.

"How long have I been sleeping?" I asked as I entered the room, feeling only slightly better.

"Not long. About an hour."

"It's starting to become a habit."

"What?"

"That someone is always trying to kill me. My body can't handle all this, yet I'm still here." My voice became louder, albeit a little shaky. "It was only an hour ago that two vampires drained me. I should be dead, Sebastian. Why aren't I dead?"

Sebastian sat and stared at me, an expression filled with either pity or sadness.

"What? Why are you giving me that look?" I could feel my face getting hot, and my hands bunched into fists. It was only when I clenched so tightly, my fingernails digging into my flesh and there was pain, that I could think clearer.

"Let me take you to Léon," Sebastian said, climbing off the bed, pulled shoes on and stood by the door.

I pulled on my shoes and ran to catch up to him.

The walls had shifted again, and the hallways were different. When we reached Léon's office, Sebastian didn't bother knocking; he opened the door, and we entered.

Léon was on the phone, he lifted a finger to let us know he was busy and pointed to the white sofas for us to sit and wait until he finished.

I didn't know why I was mad, but when I entered Léon's office and sat down, my anger started to seep away like water off my skin. I wondered whether I was always this angry.

But I had reason to be angry—Léon's friends had almost killed me. It meant that I was almost killed twice in the same week. What were the odds? I felt tired and frustrated thinking about it.

Léon ended his call and sat across from us. "Why are you so angry?"

I frowned. "How do you know I was angry? Were you reading my mind again?"

He smiled. "I can see it on your face."

"You really want to know why I'm angry?" I asked rhetorically. "Let's talk about the fact that the two of you seem to know something you aren't sharing. And then, your friends tried to kill me." I pointed my index finger at Léon.

"Please accept my humble apology. But I assure you, they are being punished."

"How?"

"We've locked them in their coffins."

"What does that mean?"

"It means they will stay there until I feel they have suffered enough. They will go without food for a very long time. I should notify the Vampire Council and have them killed, but I still have need of them."

Léon and Sebastian shared a look, talking from mind-to-mind.

"And what else?" I asked, crossing my arms in front of my chest and frowning again. I stared from one to the other, but they were still mind-talking.

Léon opened his mouth and about to say something when there was a knock on the door. "Come in," he said.

A tall man entered, wearing a brown business suit with patches at the elbows. He had brown eyes and brown hair with hints of gray on the sides that was neatly cut and styled with a side parting. His features were long to match his body, and he stood graciously near Léon.

"Kit, this is the woman you've been investigating."

I flinched.

Léon shook Kit's hand and then held his hand out to me,

palm facing up. "This is Kit, the private investigator I told you about. He has some information."

Kit gave a small bow in my direction, then said, "Nice to finally meet you. Okay, do you want the good news or the bad news?"

"Gee, I don't know, Kit. Shouldn't it all be good news, since I know nothing?" I grumbled, my anger blossoming once more.

Kit glanced at Léon before focusing back on me; he was straight-faced, showing no emotion. His beady brown eyes narrowed, he straightened his shirt and fixed his tie. He pulled a black leather notebook out of his jacket pocket and opened it toward the back.

"Right then." Kit licked his finger and pinched the page between his index finger and thumb. "Your name is Blaire Oona Thorne." He paused, glancing at Léon for a heartbeat.

Léon nodded. "Go on, Kit. Tell her. She needs to know all of it."

"For heaven's sake, will you tell me already."

"You work for Ulysses Assassins."

He stopped and stared at me. If the name was supposed to register something with me, it didn't. I shrugged.

Kit continued. "You are an assassin, Blaire. You are a hired *monster killer*. You are described as extremely dangerous."

I burst out laughing and leaned against the couch. "Is this a joke?" I sat down, pulling my knees tightly against my chest. I didn't care if my shoes were dirty on the clean white sofa. I wasn't an assassin; that's wrong. It had to be wrong. I shook my head.

"He's serious, Blaire. You kill monsters for money." Léon's face was impassive. He sat across from us with his elbows settled on his knees, his index fingers steepled, giving me his full attention. He was studying me with his blank face, but I didn't want to look at him. I turned my attention back to Kit.

Kit continued. "You started working as an assassin fifteen years ago. Your daughter…" He paused, looked at me as if waiting for my walls to crash down.

"Say again, I have a child?" I had a little girl somewhere. I smiled as tears filled my eyes, and still hugging my knees.

"Her name is Scout. She was born twelve years ago."

I continued smiling and wiping my eyes.

"But, there was an attempted kidnapping, and the man you were dating—your ex, her father—disappeared with her."

Just as my heart had risen with hope at the thought of a daughter, it was crushed in my chest hearing that someone had tried to take her away. And that because of it, they were gone. She was gone.

How could I kill people for money then went home to a child, to my family like I did nothing wrong? How was I sucked into such a fucked-up profession? I rubbed my eyes with my thumbs.

After a moment I cleared my throat and said, "Do you know who wanted to kidnap her? Why?"

"No, I couldn't find anything," Kit replied. "I tried to find them, but we can only assume that your ex changed their names. It's almost as though they've dropped off the face of the earth."

My chest tightened, my heartbeat thumping in my ears. Could I find them? Find her?

"The man you work for; his name is Marcus. He started Ulysses Assassins twenty years ago. You have a partner with whom you always do hits—Ralph—and he has worked there almost as long as you have. The torso and the severed hand we found in the trunk of your car belonged to a guy called Shane—

he had only worked with you for five years. We are still running tests on the samples we pulled, so we don't yet know how he was killed. The tests we're running should confirm if there were any traces left by the killer."

My head swam, and Kit blurred around the edges. I flew up from the sofa and darted for the dustbin near Léon's desk. What I threw up was only bile and spit.

Sebastian was right behind me holding tissues he pulled from a box on the desk. I took them to wipe my mouth, threw those dirty tissues in the bin and took a few more to dry my eyes.

I was an assassin.

I killed the monsters.

Flashes of the body from the car filled my vision and I knew him; I worked with him. And now Shane was dead.

My daughter, Scout; was gone, and it was likely that I would never see her again. I would never know what her first words were, when she had taken her first steps or how she lost her first tooth. I would never know how her first day of school went, or whether anyone was picking on her or if she was doing well?

I would never know who she was.

My shoulders slumped. I threw the last of the tissues in the bin and joined Sebastian on the sofa again.

I felt numb. I felt cold. I felt empty.

I deserved having been attacked.

I deserved to have no memory. Perhaps it was a blessing in disguise.

And I deserved to have forgotten about the family I had hurt badly enough that my daughter was almost kidnapped, and my boyfriend had left me, taking our child. For good.

I deserved it all.

The office was painfully quiet.

I heard Sebastian breathe beside me and Kit's wheezing chest. Léon took in air, even though he was a vampire and didn't need to breathe. I frowned. How could I hear these things? It wasn't something I wanted to understand at this moment. I would deal with it later.

I scowled at Léon. Were they telling me the truth about Ralph; about my daughter; about me being an assassin? They could be right about Ralph, and wrong about everything else. Ralph said I couldn't trust them. My neck stiffened, and my chest tightened.

"Now that we know who and what you are, Blaire," Léon said, breaking the silence. His voice ringing loud in my ears. "Perhaps it's possible someone tried to kill you before you were hired to kill them." He watched me with careful eyes. "Kit told me all this before he arrived, and I tried to get hold of this Marcus and Ralph so that they could come here. But the Ulysses offices are deserted, and the phone numbers don't work. It seems they have left you, Blaire." He spat out my name like poison on his tongue.

"Why are you so pissed, Léon? You aren't the one who just heard about your whole life for the first time and discovered you're a piece of crap." I said, sounding angry. I would rather be angry than sad.

Then I looked at Kit and said, "Do I have an apartment? I may have overstayed my welcome." I stood. "And can you give me a ride?"

Kit glanced from me to his master, and stuttered, "Yes," — and waited for Léon's reply.

"Do as she asks, Kit," Léon said, before turning to me. "It's not you I'm angry at, Blaire. It's the situation we all find ourselves in. You are an assassin—you kill monsters like me, monsters like Sebastian—and you are in my home. You know of

97

my businesses, and you have seen the inside of these walls." His voice grew louder with each sentence until he was practically yelling, and he threw his arms up in the air when he said, 'walls'.

I blinked at him and thought about what he said. I agreed with every word he said—I couldn't be trusted. But was I really the same person described in Kit's notebook; an assassin? I didn't feel like her.

"I don't know what to say, Léon." My voice came out strained. "I don't know what happened three nights ago. I don't know what I was working on. If my partner, Ralph, and I always worked together—then why wasn't he with me? Why wasn't he my back-up? Why was I cut up and left to die?" My throat tightened, and tears welled in my eyes. "Why was there a man's torso left in my car? I don't have the answers to any of these questions. I only have more questions." I walked to the door, opened it then stopped. "I don't even know how to get out of your fucking home!" I groaned frustratingly. "Kit, please can you take me to my apartment, now?"

"Sure." Kit fumbled in his jacket pockets, returned his notebook and fished out his car keys.

Léon's voice was deadpan. "Sebastian, go with them."

"No." I raised my hand to stop Sebastian from coming any closer. "You have done more than enough for me. If I am as dangerous as Kit describes, I will not endanger any more lives. Thank you for everything, Léon. Thank you for saving me, but it's best if I go now."

Misery enveloped me as I followed Kit out of the giant maze of a warehouse. We exited via a way I could not have predicted but at the same time impressed with how these walls kept changing, but they were fucking confusing.

Kit's car was an old nineties BMW that was well looked after and still had that new car smell, which I assumed originated from the little glass bottle hanging from the rear-view mirror.

Kit started the engine.

"I know it feels as though a ton of bricks has just been dropped on you, but give the vampire a break. You are an assassin, and he helped you without knowing that. The news caught him off guard."

"Thanks, Kit, but I don't feel like talking right now. Just get me home. Please."

Ten

My home wasn't an apartment, but a large house in an upmarket suburb; how very *Stepford* of me.

Kit was a gentleman and walked me to the front door.

"Do you have keys?" I asked him.

"No," he replied. "Let's see if you kept a spare somewhere on the porch."

We searched under the mat, above the door frame and under all the pot plants that littered the porch, but there was nothing.

I stared at the garden, which appeared as though it had once been kept neat but looked in desperate need of being watered. There was a collection of dirty little pebbles around one of the plants, and one of the pebbles looked suspiciously clean. I picked it up, finding it to be lighter than a pebble should be, and shook it. Something loosened inside. I turned it around, finding a plastic lid which I pulled open. A key fell out. I placed the plastic pebble back in its place and opened the front door.

The door opened into a living room with a floating island separating the living area from the kitchen. There was an eight-seater dining room table in the middle of the room with a couch near the window and no television. Down the hallway to the right were two spare bedrooms, a guest bathroom, and the main bedroom with an en-suite bathroom. It was homey in a suburban-wifey kind of way.

I opened all the cupboards in all the rooms, including the kitchen and bathroom, and it looked like a typical family house.

I turned to Kit as he followed me around. "If I'm such a badass assassin, where are my guns? A desk full of contracts? A range of knives on the wall or my kit?"

He shrugged.

"I thought you investigated me?"

"I did." He stepped away from me.

"But there is nothing here, Kit. No pictures or personal effects. Nothing here that tells me I even live here."

"I don't know," he said, shrugging again.

"Then leave, Kit. If you can't help me, I'd rather you leave."

"Here is my card." He handed me a gray card marked '*Kit Investigations*' on which he had scribbled his number.

"Thanks." I took his card and slipped it in my pocket. As I did so, I felt the other card; the one Ralph had given me. Maybe I could phone Ralph and ask him what was going on.

"Call me anytime, about anything—Léon will pay the bill."

"Why would I need your help and have Léon pay?"

"Just saying."

"Thanks, Kit. Now go."

When Kit left, I locked the front door and banged my head against it. The pain helped but I was nowhere near solving anything. Perhaps I needed to check the house again.

I checked the back door and found it bolted shut. Then I

rummaged through the kitchen drawers, but there was nothing out of the ordinary to be found.

When I opened the fridge, the air wafting out took my breath away. I used one hand to keep the door open and the other to cover my nose and mouth. The only items on the shelves were a Chinese takeout box, black bananas and something wrapped in tinfoil. I brought the dustbin closer and began to dispose of the spoiled food. The bananas went first. Next, I opened the lid of the tinfoil wrapping which contained green lasagne, which immediately joined the bananas. The Chinese takeout was unusually light for food, however, when I shook the contents something rattled inside. I looked the box over and saw 'Mr Ming's' logo printed on one side.

Mr Ming's. That's the restaurant near the alley where they had attacked me.

Inside the box was a roll of film, the type that needed to be handed in to be developed at a 24-hr photo shop. The fact that I had stored it in the fridge suggested I had gone to some lengths to hide it, and I intended to see what was on it as soon as I was able.

I set the film on the floating island and inspected the freezer; there was only a bag of peas, a box of fries and an ice tray inside. Nothing suspicious.

I searching the lounge, in between the cushions and in the drawers, but there was nothing untoward.

The spare bedrooms and guest bathroom were just that.

Next, I opened the closet in the main bedroom, but they contained only clothing, empty travel bags and shoes. In the en-suite bathroom, there were only toiletries.

Nothing in the entire house jumped out shouting that I was an assassin. *Nothing*.

I sat on the bed and fell backward with my arms spread

wide. The pain behind my eyes throbbed. The bedside clock read eleven in the evening. I stuck my hand between the mattress and base of the bed. On the right side, there was nothing, but on the left-hand side, there was an envelope which had an initial and a surname written on it; '*F.C. Armateurs*'.

Shit. It didn't ring any bells. It was just another question to the string of answers I didn't have.

I fished the two cards out of my pocket and searched for a phone. There was one in the kitchen between the wall and the fridge; it was an odd place to keep the phone but I thought nothing else of it. I picked up the receiver and dialed Ralph's number.

I got an answering machine and left a message. "Ralph, they say my name is Blaire. I'm at a house they say belongs to me. If you are who you say you are, can you come over? I need answers." I hung up and set the cards and envelope on the floating island next to the roll of film.

I glanced around the kitchen, then went to the back door and unlocked it. There was a small backyard with grass that needed cutting and a few overgrown shrubs. To the left was a tool shed; I nudged the door open, and inside there were only gardening tools.

The house, garden, and tool shed did not seem like a place an assassin would call home. It all seemed too normal for an assassin. There had to be another place; one an investigator, vampire or were-animal could not easily discover.

Back inside the kitchen, I locked the back door and heard floor boards creaking behind me. I spun around, and a man stood just outside the kitchen with the front door standing wide open behind him.

I froze. I didn't recognize him. His brown hair was neatly cut, and his eyes were small and blue. He had a large but flattish nose, a full bottom lip with a thinner top lip and his posture told me he was a fighter. He raised both hands in the air to show me he was unarmed. The gesture reminded me of Sebastian and the first time I met him.

The man stepped forward. "Glad to have you back, Blaire."

"Stop," I lifted my right hand with my palm facing him, and he stopped. "Who are you and how did you get in? The door was locked."

"When Ralph told me you didn't recognize him, I couldn't believe it. They really did a number on you, didn't they, Blaire? I'm Marcus. I'm a friendly. Remember?" His eyes searched mine. "Ulysses keeps a set of keys to this place, remember?" He held up his right hand to show me the set of keys looped around one of his fingers.

I frowned at him.

He seemed to be a similar height to me, which was short for a man. As I walked farther into the kitchen, someone else walked through the front door. The man looked like Ralph, from what I remembered of him from the club, except now his hair was neatly combed back with only a few loose strands in his face. He had shaved his beard except for a well-trimmed mustache, and he wore a white shirt and navy formal trousers without a jacket. He smiled when he saw me and stood beside Marcus. He was a master of disguises; at the club, he had looked rugged and someone you wanted to dodge, but now Ralph was handsome, with a dimple in his chin to complement his face.

"I'm glad you called, Blaire. You're safe with us."

Ralph reached out as though to stroke my arm, and I flinched, immediately stepping away from him. The hurt in his eyes was evident, and I felt that I somehow owed it to him to explain.

"It's not that I don't believe you—I'm having a hard time

believing anyone at the moment. Until my memory comes back, I'm keeping everyone at arm's length."

There was a strong draught and the front door slammed against the wall. Ralph closed it and approached me again. This time, I let him.

"We know, Blaire, and we will help you. We will tell you everything—but not here."

"Shh!" Marcus lifted his hand and brought one finger to his mouth. He tapped Ralph on the shoulder and motioned for him to go to a bedroom. Before they hid, he whispered to me, "Sebastian is coming. Do not let him know that we are here with you."

His words left me more confused. Apparently, Marcus and Ralph were my friends and coworkers and I should trust them. I guessed they knew me better than anyone. But how did Marcus know that Sebastian was here? And, why was Sebastian here? As I thought about it, there was a knock on the door.

I opened the door to find Sebastian standing on the porch with a bag in his hand, which he raised in my direction.

"What do you want?" I asked, not taking the bag out of his hand.

"I brought you the clothes Léon bought for you. I thought you could use them." I narrowed my eyes. "I don't mean any harm. I just came by to give you the bag," Sebastian said, sounding hurt.

"Why bother? It's only clothes." I crossed my arms in front of my chest.

He fidgeted with the strap and stepped inside. I didn't try to stop him, which was a surprise even to me.

"Why did you really come, Sebastian? I have my own clothes." I gave him a deadpan expression.

He dropped the bag next to my feet, and as I glanced down

at it, he moved. He was so quick I didn't comprehend what he was doing until Sebastian cupped my face with his large hands and kissed me. His lips were soft and warm against mine. My lips parted. He explored the inside of my mouth, hard, like he could kiss right through and come out the other side.

I uncrossed my arms and wrapped them around his waist. Things tightened down below, and I wanted to touch more skin; my hands moved under his shirt and felt his muscles move beneath my fingers. He was hot to the touch. He pulled me closer; my body touched the line of his body, and I could feel how happy he was to be here. His hands moved down my back, trailing lower to cup my ass, and a moan formed in my mouth.

He stopped kissing, and we stopped touching.

I stared at him breathlessly, my mouth parted, wanting to touch more of him. All of him.

He smiled like a naughty schoolboy, which made me smile, too.

"Oh," I said, touching my lips, still wet from his kiss. I licked my lips. "As much as I enjoyed that and want more, I can't. Not now. I need to sort out a few things first," I said, stepping closer to him until our bodies touched once more. My hands went to his chest and then around his waist, and pressed one side of my face against his chest. I hugged him and the tension in my shoulders dissolved, and a sigh escaped my lips. I felt calm in the circle of his arms. I pressed my ear over his heart and listened to its rapid beating. His grip tightened around me, and he kissed the top of my head.

"I know." He pulled away and kissed me chastely on the lips. "We are here for you if you need our help. Any time. Ask any taxi driver to bring you to the club; they'll know the way. You are always welcome... Blaire." His smile reached his eyes.

It felt strange hearing Sebastian use my name, especially as we had spent the past few days absolutely oblivious to it, but there was something in the mischievous way in which he said it that made me like it all the more.

We kissed again, and he left.

Eleven

I watched Sebastian climb into a dark-colored car and drive away. I shivered, and something ached in the pit of my stomach.

"God, woman! What's with you and this man?" Marcus said as he came around the corner, laughing.

I ignored his comment; I could explain to him how I had survived, but it was none of his business. I picked up the bag of clothing and threw it onto the sofa. Marcus headed into the kitchen and stood beside the fridge. Ralph stood next to me as Marcus pulled something behind the fridge and stepped out of the way. The fridge moved forward on some kind of system—I didn't know how, or at least not one I remembered—to reveal a small opening in the floor. Marcus stepped down into the opening and disappeared, then a light illuminated the space below.

"What is that?"

"One of our home-bases." Ralph followed Marcus down the opening.

I wrapped my arms around my body and hunched forward, peering through the opening. There were stairs going down into a secret basement.

"Come, precious; we don't have all night," Marcus yelled.

I rolled my eyes and descended the stairs. At the bottom, I felt my mouth slacken. The room was large. There were four single beds to the left, each covered with a blue sheet and a matching blanket. There was an armory cage against the far wall and two black leather sofas. In between the sofas, there was a pool table with colorful balls precisely positioned ready for a game to start. To my right, also against the wall, was a fridge, a table with little containers and a freezer next to that.

Marcus leaned against the wall near the stairs and pressed a button. There were sounds above me; I looked up and watched how the fridge started moving back in place and the door slid closed. We were safely hidden away. I walked around the cement column and in the far lefthand side, near the four beds, was a toilet and shower with a wall up to my shoulders enclosing it.

"Fuck me," I said, as I walked around the room and stopped in front of the armory cage. Locked inside, there was every kind of weapon; machine guns, shotguns, handguns, knives—all shapes and sizes—and enough bullets to supply an army. "I knew upstairs looked too plain and boring for an assassin, but this—this is fucking *crazy*. Do we all share this place?"

"Glad to hear you still cuss like a sailor, Blaire," Marcus said. "And no, we don't. Below each of our houses is a room like this one. It's for those situations where one of us has been compromised; we can still go to any of the other basements."

Ralph sat on one sofa and took a manilla folder from the floor. He opened it, and his face held no emotion yet I could see in his eyes the seriousness with which the conversation would turn. Shit. I wanted to know. I *needed* to know. But would the information change the person I was now?

Ralph motioned with his head for me to sit beside him. "You still want to know everything, Blaire?"

I sat next to him, bent my right leg and rested it on the sofa, and turned my body to face him.

He waited for me to settle down, opened the folder on his lap, and began removing documents and photos.

"This is your daughter, Scout. She is twelve and lives with Mason. These pictures were taken when they were still living in California."

He handed me a picture of Scout and Mason; they were laughing while walking in a park, wearing sunglasses, and Scout was holding a leash for a golden retriever. It felt strange seeing a picture of an ex I simply couldn't remember, and a daughter I couldn't believe was my own. I couldn't clearly see their faces because the photo had been taken from a distance.

"They are safe; they have new identities, and we are the only ones who know where that information is kept. You sealed it in a safe deposit box at your bank, and you are the only one with a key to open it."

A key. Could it be the one that Sebastian and I had found in the alley—the key chain with the hieroglyphics? I felt my jean pocket, and it was still there. It relieved me, but that would only last if one of the keys opened that safe deposit box.

Ralph gave me a document. Something about it felt familiar; a distant calling from my memory that I couldn't quite yet hear. My eyes scanned the page.

It was a contract order—and it named Léon as the target.

"Shit." The surprise on my face must have shown.

"Exactly," Ralph said. "We—you and I—were supposed to

kill Léon on the night you were attacked. But before we get to that, let me explain the reason why he was the target."

Shock still held me in its grip, but I managed to mutter the words, "Okay, go ahead."

"Léon owns a shipping company, 'F.C. *Armateurs*'."

I flinched at the name; it was the name from the envelope I'd found tucked between the base of the bed and the mattress.

Ralph inclined his head as he noticed my reaction. Rather than calling me out on it, he continued speaking, allowing me the time to process what he was telling me on my own. "They handled a large shipment from Egypt, which is of interest to us and has mysteriously disappeared. This also happened on the night of your attack."

"What was in the actual shipment?"

"I was getting to that," — he elbowed me, — "we were given a month to conduct reconnaissance, and then we had to kill Léon or give up the cash to fund handing the contract over to another assassin. We were hired because of something in that shipment."

Ralph glanced at Marcus, who was sitting across from us on the other sofa. "Marcus followed Sebastian and Léon, but he could never get a set schedule; they were always doing different things at different times, which made it harder for us to track them. Léon was also never alone. Sebastian and Miles was always with him. When Marcus first saw Miles, he had to backpedal somewhat because Miles's brother Danny is a were-lion—just like Marcus."

"You are a were-lion?" I spluttered. All these were-animals revealing themselves was fast becoming the only constant in my life.

Marcus nodded. "You don't remember that either, do you?"

"No, sorry, I don't." To Ralph, I said, "Are you a were-anything?"

Ralph shook his head. "No, I am simply a mortal human like yourself." His eyes were teasing, and his smile was wicked.

"Okay, then what happened?"

"When Marcus realized who Miles was, he was afraid that Miles would recognize him and tell Danny, which meant he could only follow them at a distance. Obviously, that didn't help us very much. You and I, meanwhile, were tracking the shipment, and we discovered that it contained the mummy of Amenemhat. Where Egypt is concerned, there's always bound to be a curse or some such malediction attached to it." He smiled and shook his head, but something in the way Ralph had spoken the words told me he wasn't joking.

"So, anyway, rumor has it that Amenemhat was discovered near King Tutankhamun's tomb in the Valley of the Kings, near Luxor. Egyptologists claim that he was buried with three jewels of extreme power, but no records exist detailing their exact strength. Somehow, Léon learned of the discovery and tried to ship it over, but it would appear that someone close to him is prepared to kill him over these jewels. We don't know who this person is or what these jewels can do, but I think you found out, and consequently, they tried to kill you." Ralph's gaze held sadness, and he touched my cheek gently.

I didn't push him away; I closed my eyes, smelling the soap he used and his aftershave; a blend of cedarwood, oak and vanilla. His smell was familiar and comforting.

I frowned at him. "Are we an item? I mean, are we together... romantically?"

He pulled his hand away. It was clear that the sudden way in which I had asked the question threw him slightly, but that didn't stop him from answering. "No. You didn't want to complicate things, so we ended it before it even began."

It made sense; as the old saying goes, never mix business with pleasure.

"Okay," I said. I needed to understand as much as possible. "So, instead of Léon having the jewels, someone else knew about them and tried to kill him to take them for themselves." I had been living in Léon's house for the past few days, and the person who had hired me had not made themselves known. None of it made sense. "Do you think Léon knows all this?"

"I think he knows something. I mean he has to know. After all, from what we can tell, he has tripled the amount of guards protecting him."

"Now I understand why he seemed to freak out when he heard I was an assassin."

Ralph shrugged. "So, this is where we are. Someone hired us to kill Léon, someone tried to kill you, and now the mummy and the jewels are gone. Does this ring any bells?"

I sighed. "No. I don't remember any of it, and the way I feel right now, I don't think I have it in me to assassinate anyone."

My chest tightened, and so I sat back into the sofa, allowing the soft cushion to comfort me. Moving around on the sofa sent the keys digging into my thigh. I pulled them out.

"I have these keys," I said, showing them to Ralph. "Sebastian found them in the alley where I was attacked. We thought they might be mine. We also found a car that might belong to me. There was a torso in the trunk." Hairs rose at the back of my neck, and a shiver went down my spine like a block of ice. The thought of the grisly discovery of the mutilated body still haunted me.

"That was Shane." Ralph sighed. "He was a good kid, but he wasn't one for taking orders. Marcus told him to follow you while I was following the shipment. I'm sorry that they chopped him up, but he almost got you killed, Blaire." Ralph closed the folder and threw it on the floor near his feet. "He should have kept you safe, but he didn't."

I frowned. "What was I doing in that area, anyway?"

"You were following Léon because Marcus had other business to attend to."

I remembered the Chinese container from the fridge. "I found some things hidden upstairs. Do you think they might be connected?" I started to get the sense that I already knew the answer.

"What things?" Marcus asked. He had been so quiet that I had forgotten he was there.

"In the fridge, there was a roll of film in a 'Mr. Ming's' Chinese takeout container, and under the bed, between the mattress and the base, was an envelope with 'F.C. Armateurs' written on it. That's the name of Léon's shipping company, right?"

Ralph nodded, but it was Marcus who said, "That's right. Do you know what's on the roll of film?"

"No. We need to have it developed somewhere."

"I can do it. Where are the items now?"

"Both are on the floating island in the kitchen."

Marcus stood and Ralph said, "Where are you going, Marcus? It's late in the evening and nowhere will be open. We can organize developing the film tomorrow." Ralph also got to his feet. "First, we need to discuss our next steps and find out who is behind all this, Marcus."

Marcus sighed, relenting. It was the right call, and he knew it.

Since they were standing, I also stood.

Ralph passed me to approach Marcus, who said, "You are right, Ralph. Where do you suggest we start?"

I moved toward them and yawned, wiping sleepy tears out my eyes, and said, "Guys, it's late and I'm tired. How about we get some sleep first and decide what to do next in the morning?"

"If it's fine with you, can we stay here for the night?" Ralph asked. "It would be easier if we stayed together, then we can get an early start in the morning."

"Uh, okay. It's fine with me," I said, still a little untrusting. I supposed I could always grab a knife from the cage to sleep with.

Marcus nodded. "Sure, let's sleep and then decide." He disappeared in the general direction of the bathroom.

Ralph stayed beside me.

"Who do you think is behind it, Ralph?" I asked him, touching his elbow so that he would look at me.

"I honestly don't know," he replied. "Whoever it is has been very careful not to show themselves."

"Who sends us the contracts?"

His eyes brightened. "Just guess what the name of the company is."

"The suspense is killing me, Ralph. Just spit it out."

"Slayerbody."

"You're kidding."

"No." He yawned and walked over to the beds. "We can look into them tomorrow, too."

Marcus finished in the bathroom and sat on the bed on the far left nearest to it.

After my bathroom break, I had two choices of beds: either of the two beds in the middle. Marcus was next to the wall on the left, and Ralph was on the right. I took the one closest to Ralph.

Neither man was under their blankets, and both of them faced the wall.

"How do I switch off the lights?" I asked.

Ralph clapped twice, and the overhead light immediately cut out. I kicked off my shoes and climbed into bed.

Twelve

I awoke to the sound of beans grinding and the smell of coffee. The room was bright. I held my hand over my eyes and sat up to see what was going on. The beds where the men had slept were neatly made; I guess sleeping on top of the blankets helped. My bed, on the other hand, looked properly slept in.

"Is it 'good morning' or 'good afternoon'?" I said as I sat beside Marcus on the sofa.

"It's only 08:25 a.m." Ralph handed me a cup of coffee. The mug was pastel pink and bore the image of a woman on its front beside the words '*Ulysses Assassins*'. Neat; we had our own personalized mugs. Maybe it had been Ralph's idea for a novelty gift.

"Okay," Marcus said and placed his mug—a pastel blue variant of my own, except with a man on the front with '*Ulysses Assassins*' dripping in blood—on the floor by his feet. "I was thinking about what we need to do. I will drop the film off and try to find our vampire friends; see if one of them goes off by themselves. Meanwhile, you two can check out Slayerbody."

"Sure. A name like 'Slayerbody' is bound to be just an avatar, but there are ways we can trace the source," Ralph said with confidence. "I just need to look."

"Is that what you do in our work partnership?" I asked.

"Yup, but all that equipment is back at my place. We can go after we're done with our coffee."

I nodded. "Sounds like a plan. How do we usually keep in touch with one another?"

"Cellphones."

"Where's mine?"

"Gone. I tried searching for you by triangulating your phone the night you were attacked, but I couldn't pick up your signal. Whoever hurt you must have smashed the phone and dumped it."

"Where did you look for me?"

"There was a spot near the laundromat that we always used for meets. I looked there for you the next day, but all I found was a pool of blood. I called around to try and find you, but there was no mention of a Jane Doe at any of the hospitals or morgues."

"Did you search the entire alley?"

He nodded.

"That's where Sebastian found this key chain." I reached into the pocket of my jeans and lifted the key chain with the three keys. "I don't know where he found it."

"I don't know. I didn't see it there when I looked."

Hmm, I would have to ask Sebastian exactly where he had found the key chain. It was strange that Ralph hadn't seen it first if he had been there before us.

I took another sip of my coffee.

Having rinsed his now empty mug in the bathroom sink, Marcus set it back on the table near the fridge and said, "I'm going to head out. Call me if you come up with anything."

"Will do," Ralph said. "What about tonight? Are we meeting up again?" He stood to clean his mug, which had the same design as Marcus's but was in green.

"No, let's reconvene tomorrow sometime. I'll call later with what I find."

"Okay." Ralph placed his mug on the table next to Marcus's.

Marcus pressed the button by the stairs to activate the opening. Once the mechanism had moved the fridge aside, he climbed the stairs and then was gone.

I found my eyes were lingering on the opening. "How do we know that there isn't someone up there waiting for us?"

"I am glad to hear your instincts are still functioning properly." Ralph sat beside me again with a teasing grin.

Nice to know I was amusing.

Sensing that I still needed reassurance, Ralph elaborated. "We have motion sensors and trigger alarms scattered throughout the house, and also out back and in front."

"Oh, cool."

A moment passed, and then I asked, "How did you know that I would be at the club?"

"I didn't. When you and Shane went missing, I found your car still in that parking area. I knew then that something bad had happened. When I saw the blood in the alley, I suspected that it belonged to you. With no way of finding you, I focused on the last link I had to your disappearance; I kept watch on Léon and Sebastian." He exhaled. "Something told me that you were still alive. So, I waited, and then I saw you with Sebastian. When the two of you were walking toward the alley, you looked so confused and scared—I'd never seen you like that before. Ever.

"I suspected that your memory might have failed in the way you were acting, and I didn't think that you would remember me. But I was so glad to see you alive. That left me in an awkward position; if you didn't recognize me, I couldn't exactly jump out of hiding. So, I watched you, and I saw you collapse in the park near your car. I was watching when they fetched you with a van and took you back to the warehouse. I knew that they were looking after you. If they wanted to hurt you, you would've been dead already. When I heard everybody was going to the club, I hoped that you would too. Then, when I saw you, I took a chance when you were alone. Sorry I scared you."

"Yeah, you did, but I guess it was necessary." I tried for a smile, but the corners quivered. I stared at the far wall beyond the beds and felt empty. "What was I like?" I asked, without looking back at him. "I mean, do I still seem like the same person?"

Ralph considered my question for a moment, then answered, "You are different. You used to be tougher; now you seem… calmer. Softer. If I'm honest, before we get in too deep following any leads, you could probably benefit from a refresher." He smiled. "When we get to my place, we can test your muscle memory. We can run through a few weapons tests; I'll show you the ones you would normally use, and then we can take it from there." He touched the wound above my eye, which made me look directly at him. "They properly messed you up, and yet it looks great after only four days. Does it still hurt?"

"No." I wasn't sure whether to tell him about the vampire mark that Léon had left and how it had helped me to heal quicker. In truth, I wasn't sure what the mark really meant; I definitely needed to find out more about it. Perhaps that's why I was so angry at Sebastian and Léon—the fact that they hadn't fully explained it to me. What I needed was to find another vampire who would.

I lifted my shirt to show Ralph my side. I stood so that he could better see my injury.

"Fuck, Blaire! They tore you in half."

I was close enough to see his blue eyes darken as his pupils dilated. He traced the pink scars lightly with his warm fingers and followed the smaller scars as they split off from the larger one.

I giggled and pulled my shirt down. "That tickles."

"I'm sorry I wasn't there to help you." I could see only honesty and sorrow in his eyes.

"It wasn't your fault, Ralph."

"Yes, it was. We always work together, Blaire; we are a team. The one night we didn't, you almost get killed. So, it is my fault." He stood, and the look in his eyes still spoke of sadness. I wanted to take that sadness from his face, but I just didn't know how.

So, I did the one thing I could. I hugged him.

Thirteen

I packed an overnight bag with fresh clothes and locked the front door. Ralph drove to his place, and as it turned out, our houses were about twenty minutes apart with no traffic. His house was styled similarly to mine, except it smelled like a man's house; a mixture of aftershave, gym bag, sweat and musk. But, as I stood beside Ralph waiting for his fridge to slide away from the wall, his scent was familiar and made me feel safe. My face was near his chest, and I knew his smell; cedarwood, oak and vanilla with a hint of sweat. I must've worked with that smell around me for years, and I knew in my heart that we were best friends.

My heart also suggested that I had probably slept with him at least once, too.

I also remembered Sebastian's smell, a combination of the ocean and extravagant French eau de toilette, from the few times he had laid beside me and held me in bed. He represented the potential for something new, exciting and promising.

Ralph didn't smell like that; Ralph smelled like home, like a comfort blanket you rushed to when scared. He was the cup of hot chocolate to soothe nerves or a good book when it rained or snowed.

I knew that I couldn't ignore that feeling. I needed to ask him about it; to explore it a little. Whatever had happened between us was beginning to feel real the more time I spent with him, even though I couldn't fully explain why.

"Before, you said we stopped before we even started. What did you mean by that?"

"We had worked together for a few years when we finally admitted that there was an attraction between us, but you didn't want either of us to get hurt. You didn't want others to know that they could use one of us against the other. It could've gotten both of us killed. So, we only had that one night together, and since then, we've been the best of friends." He motioned for the opening in the floor and descended the stairs.

I knew it; he was my comfort, my home. I placed my hand on his shoulder and followed him into the darkness until we reached the bottom of the stairs. I let go of his shoulder when we reached the floor, and he switched on the light and closed the latch. Bright stars flickered before my eyes, and it took a couple of seconds to get used to the fluorescent lights overhead.

"Are there any photo albums I can browse through? Anything else that might reveal my past or tell me what I was like?"

"There are no photos, no albums, nothing that would tell others who you are or what you were like. We are all ghosts, Blaire; we are nobody. We are untraceable. Do you understand?" He voice raised. "You can't be the boogeyman and kill people for a living and expect to have a family photo album that's full of smiles." He sounded bitter and full of regret.

"What made you do this job?" I asked. "Did Marcus pull you in, or was it something you wanted to do? How can we do this for a living, Ralph? I mean, seriously? It's exactly as you said— we are the boogeymen. How on earth can we want to be like this?" My voice had risen, and I sounded angry. In the back of my mind, the words *'monster killer'* sounded on repeat, spoken in Kit's officious, matter-of-fact tone.

Ralph realized that he had pushed my buttons. "Sorry, I shouldn't have yelled at you. I know you are trying to sort through some things, but we are assassins, Blaire. I don't know your story... your real story; we don't know that side of each other. I only know enough for us to be able to work together at Ulysses. It's how Marcus wanted things."

He was right. I was naïve to think that he would have more information on me besides what he knew during our time working together.

I was an assassin. I was a trained killer. A ghost.

"Fine." I folded my arms across my chest. "What did you want to show me?"

Ralph's basement was a replica of mine, except for a table next to the armory cage on which a laptop, a desktop and four monitors were set. It was a techie's wet dream. The powerful desktop and the rugged laptop clearly meant serious business.

I dropped my overnight bag near one of the beds and stood by the table. "Well, then; get on with it. Search for Slayerbody, and let's see what we are up against."

"Maybe tone down the bitchiness. At least that side of you hasn't changed at all."

I froze and blinked at him. "Sorry," I muttered under my breath. I exhaled a frustrated breath and waited for Ralph to get comfortable in his chair.

He sat on his leather chair and started hitting keys, the monitors flaring to life with numbers and words flying across the screen. The search would take a while, and my body felt sticky. I pulled clothing and a towel out from my overnight bag and went to the little bathroom to shower. The water took forever to warm up, but when it did, I stood under the hot spray for a while. I washed my hair and body and let the hot water beat down on my skin until I was pink. My skin burned when I switched the water off, but the cool air began to caress me. The wall was also shoulder-height for me, so I could see Ralph tinkering away at his desk.

He could be an ass, but then again, so was I. I didn't know why I was angry at him. I felt grumpy and angry at everything and everyone.

I dried my body and dressed in fresh underwear, the same jeans and a clean navy t-shirt. I wrapped the towel around my wet hair and applied face cream and deodorant. At last, I felt human again.

My stomach made gargling sounds as I exited the bathroom. "Do you have any food upstairs we can eat? I'm hungry."

Ralph turned in his chair. "There's nothing upstairs, but you can alway have a look in the fridge down here. There must be something you can eat. But whatever you have, you have to make for me, too," he said with half a smile and a wink.

The pink mug at my place should have given it away. Why was the woman always the one to make the food? I shook my head, but I also couldn't help smiling.

I opened the fridge to find it full of food, and my mouth watered. I grabbed two small tubs of strawberry yoghurt and a loaf of bread, a tub of butter, cheese and cold meats to make the sandwiches. He had paper plates stacked on the table beneath a butter knife. I found mustard stashed in the fridge's door and made the best sandwiches ever—or, at least, I thought so.

I set his sandwich on a paper plate and placed it with a yoghurt on his desk; he thanked me and started eating. I sat on the sofa in such a way that I could still see his monitors, put my feet up on its arm, propped the paper plate on my lap and enjoyed my sandwich.

I awoke lying on my right-hand side, drool all over my hand and the paper plate on the floor. Alongside the plate was the uneaten tub of yoghurt lying upside down, its contents spilled on the floor. I sat up, lifted the tub onto the paper plate and threw it away. Grabbing a few paper towels, I cleaned the spillage, and when I finished, I glanced at Ralph's desk. It was empty, as were the bathroom and the four beds.

I spun around. Shit. Where was he?

I threw the dirty paper towels away and walked toward his desk. Ralph jumped in front of me from a crouching position behind the sofa and slapped me in the face. It stung and brought a tear to my eye. He planted his feet in a fighting position and started bouncing on the balls of his feet.

I turned with my left shoulder facing him, pretending to kick him with my left leg but instead connecting my left fist with his jaw. I moved forward, and with my right hand, I hit him flat-handed in his solar plexus, winding him. He doubled over and crashed to the floor, but he somehow jumped up almost immediately. His smile widened and held a hint of mockery.

I narrowed my eyes at him and went in for another hit. He blocked it with his right arm and used his left fist to hit me on my right side, striking the soft tissue between my hip and ribs. I doubled over and fell to my knees. There was too much pain shooting up my spine and into the base of my skull, and I fell on my ass, hugging my waist.

"Shit, shit, shit. Are you okay?" Ralph's concern sounded genuine. "I didn't hit your left-hand side. I thought you had healed."

It wasn't his fault; it was intended as good practice, and I had to admit that it was. At least we had ascertained I still knew how to fight. That said, the pain was intense. Goosebumps raised the hairs on my arms, and pain shot up my spine like a lightning bolt. The sensation was so acute that I had to fight for breath.

He held a hand out to me. "Good fight, though. Once you're stronger, we can go at it again. I don't want to damage you today. I only just got you back."

I wiped tears from my eyes and took his hand, but pain immediately shot from my shoulder and ran down my side. I fell back onto the floor, screaming loudly.

"I need help, Ralph. Fuck. There's something wrong; it's never been this painful before, and it's not easing."

Sweat beaded on my face as Ralph grabbed his cell phone. He dialed a number and spoke hurriedly to someone, asking if they were available for a house call. He nodded fast and stared at me, said thanks and hung up.

"She's coming. She will know what to do."

"Who is?"

"You won't remember her anyway, so it doesn't help to explain. I will when she gets here, though. I promise. Can I help you to a bed?"

"Please."

Ralph sat on his haunches behind me, hooked his arms under my own and lifted me up. I screamed again, but he carried on pulling me up as slowly as he could. I stared at my stomach to see if my guts were spilling out, but it only felt like my insides were being torn apart. I began to pant, my breath short and shallow. Stars twinkled in the air above me, and darkness clouded my vision.

I couldn't keep my eyes open. I couldn't stop the pain.

I fell into the murkiness of sleep.

Fourteen

I heard whispering. There was no pain, except on my right hand. Attached to it was an intravenous line with red stuff going inside me. The whispering stopped. A hand touched my left shoulder, and Ralph's face came into view, his expression filled with concern.

"How are you feeling?" he said, his smile faltering.

"What's wrong, Ralph? You look like someone's died."

He sobered. "You almost died, Blaire. If Désiré hadn't gotten here in time, you would have."

A woman stood beside Ralph and held my right hand. She was warm to the touch. "Ralph told me about the attack, and I was telling him that whoever it was, they're cursed."

I frowned. "Cursed? What makes you say that?"

"When were-animals attack humans, tests will come back with a positive or negative result, but the color of their blood stays red. Your blood is black, Blaire. I'm still waiting for the results of your bloodwork to come back, but I've started you on a transfusion regardless of the result. What I'm trying to tell you is that your blood was poisoned, and it's slowly killing you."

Her eyes flittered to the blood bag and then back to me. She was about fifty years old, with straight black hair that reached down to her waist. She had small, dark eyes, and in them, I couldn't make out where the pupil ended and the iris began. Along with crow's feet, there were also lines next to her thin lips, and she had a sharp chin and a button nose. Short and petite, her full height barely reached Ralph's shoulders.

She wore a white blouse with black dots and a colorful skirt. Tied to her forehead was a headscarf which kept her long hair back from her face. Her appearance seemed to remind me of a traveling gypsy.

As I focused on her, I came to realize that the dots of her white blouse were not an intentional pattern. Instead, it was haphazardly covered in splotches of a deep red or black. Unfortunately, the color was becoming all too familiar to me.

"Yes, this is what your blood looks like." She touched the dark marks on her blouse.

"I'm sorry I ruined your top."

She smiled and held my hand again. Tiny pinpricks traveled up my arm, gently at first but then started to burn. Her power spread throughout my body, and it made me gasp, the air sucked out of my lungs. I pulled my hand out of hers, and it was only then that I could breathe again.

"Why did you do that?" I said, rubbing my hands. "I couldn't breathe."

"You felt all of it?"

"Yes."

"That's very interesting, Blaire; I wasn't sure you would. You may not remember me, but this isn't the first time we've met, and when I saw how different your aura was, I knew I had to try. It's unusual for a human to feel power, from a vampire or a witch, like you just did. Either you are a vampire or a witch and have powers, or you don't—it should be that simple. But," Désiré said, considering me. "I've only read about a handful of humans who were able to feel and use power against whoever was pushing it into them. If I'm remembering correctly, the last human recorded to have this ability was alive in the 1600s."

I shook my head a little too quickly and stopped before I threw up. "I don't understand. What do you mean?"

"Your aura shines bright white, Blaire."

When I didn't answer her, she said to Ralph, "Do you remember her being able to feel power or magic?"

"No. In all the years I've known her, she never mentioned she could sense any power. Ever. And no one picked up on it if she could."

Désiré smiled mysteriously. "I didn't pick up on it, either. Well, my dear, it would seem that you have been hiding a special gift."

Now felt as good a time as any to come clean. "There is something I need to tell you about which may have caused this. The vampire, Léon—in order to save my life, he had to mark me. He made me his human servant. Could that have caused whatever I have now?"

I watched for Ralph's reaction, but there was none.

"No, my dear; a vampire's mark works differently. It will give you certain benefits such as healing properties derived from their life essence, but it won't give you what you have. If my thinking is correct, you can syphon power and use it later— but don't quote me. Let me find out the specifics, and I'll get back to you?"

"Please, that would be great." It felt good to hear someone referring to my newfound abilities in an almost authoritative way. At least someone was able to quantify them. I wasn't entirely reassured, though. "Is the poison out of my system now?" I asked, staring at the bag beside me.

"No, you will need to receive a transfusion every day or, failing that, every second day. The poison is so severe that I couldn't detect that a vampire had marked you." Désiré's expression became pensive. "Perhaps if the vampire was to finish the ritual and gave you the second mark, it might stop the poison and remove the curse."

"No, that is not an option." No way in hell was that happening. "I don't want the second mark. I don't want to go to him for help again. Not if I can help it."

"Then the only alternative, is to find the were-animal who bit you. You need them to tell you who it was that cursed them, so that the witch responsible can undo it. Only that witch can remove your curse; unfortunately, there's no way I can, even if I wanted to."

Dammit.

"Do you have any spare blood packs for me so I can do this myself?" I glanced at the medical items strewn on the bed beside me.

"Not on me, but I can get more from the hospital. Ralph knows where I work. Stop by when you need, and I can set it up for you." She looked me straight in the eye. "You have lost a lot of blood the last couple of days, Blaire. I have given Ralph a course of tablets for you; take them, or you will stay weak." She nodded firmly. "When you come to the hospital, I will supply you with more."

"Thank you, Désiré."

Désiré shifted uncomfortably on the balls of her feet. "Oh and Blaire? I'm sorry I can't remove the curse. Whoever conjured the curse, used a dark spell that's forbidden and punishable by death. To undo the curse, the same dark spell must be used." Her voice was grave. "Once you know who did this, give me their name."

"If you need an assassin, Désiré, you know who to call. We'll even do it for free," Ralph smirked.

"Thanks, Ralph, but it will be best if we handle it." She laughed and squeezed his shoulder. "The witch responsible needs to be taught a lesson, and for an example to be made of them to the rest of the covens." Her eyes sparkled. "Sometimes, there are worse things than death."

Shit. I would hate to be on her bad side.

Désiré kissed the air beside Ralph's cheeks and touched my hand one last time. I felt her power flare through me like ice and fire; hot and cold, all at once.

Désiré left me with a handful of vitamins and some saline solution to keep me hydrated. She waved goodbye as Ralph led her back upstairs.

I honestly didn't know what Léon would do if I went back to him and asked that he finish the ritual to see if it would help save my life. Would he even care? Would he bother completing the ritual knowing I could turn around and kill him? I was a danger; not only to him, but also to his little empire. I doubted he would help keep someone like me—an assassin—alive.

If I died, he could simply pull power from all his little vamps and still survive. He had been right, all those nights ago. I had no power to offer him in return.

The only thing left to do was to find my attacker, learn the truth behind their curse, locate the witch who had invoked it and have them remove its effects from me. But I could only solve one problem at a time. I needed to drink my vitamins, eat and then get some sleep.

Ralph descended the stairs and closed the latch. He went directly to his desk, sat down and began typing on his keyboard.

I sat up slowly, still light-headed from the transfusion, and then I tried standing, leaning against the intravenous stand. When I didn't fall over, I dragged the drip over to Ralph. When I touched his shoulder, he flinched, and I recoiled.

"Sheesh, someone's skittish! What's wrong?" I asked, staring at the monitors. Open on the screen was a search engine through which he was researching *'vampire mark'*. My interest was immediately piqued. "Oh, what does it say?" I kept my hand on his shoulder, noticing he didn't shoo me away.

"Not much. There's not much definitive information out there about vampire marks and human servants. Fair amount of speculation—but nothing really to sink your teeth into." We both smiled at his poor attempt at humor. As much as I felt it myself, I could sense his frustration behind the words, and he felt tense beneath my hand.

I let go of the drip and started rubbing his shoulders, kneading the tight knots in his muscles. He relaxed and started to read out loud.

"The first mark sets the groundwork for the vampire to assess whether the human is compatible with the process. The vampire shares power through a single bite, and thus the first mark on the human remains. Afterward, vampiric abilities are continually shared, but only up to a point. The main one is healing, but there can be some invasion of the mind and dreams.

"If the vampire is happy with their little human, they can instigate the second mark. This ritual is formal and gruesome; the vampire makes a cut near their own heart, and the human drinks from the wound. Consumption of the vampire's blood solidifies the bond between master and servant, and the vampire's power is further absorbed by the human, completing the ritual. In this way, the human gains all the benefits of being a vampire without bursting into flames."

I stopped massaging Ralph's back. "Are you serious?" I flashed back to my dream of both Léon and Sebastian—how they had both opened a vein for me to drink their blood, and that it was Sebastian who had forced his blood into my mouth. The memory of it sliding down my throat like a knife slicing along my spine. I shuddered.

"And—drum roll, please. The bond is a double-edged sword. As the human shares the vampire's unique power, if the vampire can cause fear, then so can the human. As a result, the vampire cannot punish their human servant, for doing so ends up with the vampire punishing themselves. Unless, of course, they happen to be a sadistic bastard, as most vampires already are."

"Okay, enough of that. I've already told you I won't be going back to Léon to beg him for the second mark, anyway." The thought of it was turning my stomach, so I decided to move the conversation along. "Did you learn anything about Slayerbody while I was sleeping?" I said, watching his face.

"I couldn't get in." Ralph stared at me. A hint of concern flashed in his eyes. "I couldn't bypass their security without being detected."

"Please tell me there is another plan somewhere in there?" I tapped the side of his head playfully.

"Not at the moment."

"Now what?"

"Now, you need to rest. Besides, we can't do anything until that blood bag is empty."

I leered at the bag; it was only half empty. My movement was too quick, and bright sparkly stars came into view. My right hand grabbed Ralph's chair, and my left grabbed the stand connected to the drip. Ralph stood and held me up under my arms, which felt awkward because he was facing me.

"I'm all right," I said, stepping backward and out of his arms. "Let me lie down for a little while. Maybe you should phone Marcus and hear how his day is going?"

Ralph pulled out his cellphone, searched for Marcus's number and started pacing on the other side of the room.

While I was back in bed, Ralph had spoken to Marcus and came to stand at the footboard. He seemed concerned or as though he was in disbelief. I wasn't sure which, and it took a while before he explained.

"What's wrong, Ralph?"

"I don't know, but something weird is going on with Marcus. He says he isn't feeling well, but he's a were-lion, for goodness' sake. Were-animals never get sick, except when they're injured through fighting—but even then, they can heal themselves. And the process is quick, too." He furrowed his brows. "Anyway, he says the photo place is open until ten tonight and asked if we could fetch the prints. He will arrange for us to collect them with the manager; that way, we don't have to go all the way to his place to fetch the stub."

"What are you worried about?"

Ralph rubbed his chin. "I don't know. It reminds me of the night you were attacked, and how he asked Shane to be your backup. I've only just realized, but I don't actually know what he was doing while we were all busy."

I wasn't sure what to make of that. Not remembering Marcus at all prior to the last few days meant I wasn't in the best place to gauge whether his behavior was normal or not. But I had to agree with Ralph; were-animals didn't fall ill. Ever.

Something must have shown on my face that mirrored

Ralph's because he gave a slight nod of his head, as if we were thinking the same thing.

"You think he is up to something, too?" Ralph said.

"Maybe, I don't know, or rather I don't remember what he's like. How about we fetch the photos first and then go around to his place?"

"Sure. Grab your pills and bring your blood bag along; I'll hook it up in the car."

Once we were in the car, Ralph hooked my intravenous on the little handle above the passenger-side door as I buckled into my seat. Ralph drove us to the photo place and found a parking spot close to the entrance. I asked him to get me something to snack on if we were going to be following our boss around all night, and I stayed in the car while he collected the photos.

Ralph returned after twenty minutes with a bag that he dumped in my lap. As he started the engine, I drank the water he had purchased, and it was cool against my throat. With the back of my hand, I felt my forehead.

"Do I have a temperature? I feel hot."

Ralph almost backhanded me in the face trying to feel my forehead. I guided his hand to my head.

"Yeah, you feel hot. Did you bring the tablets Désiré left for you?"

I set the bag down on the floor between my legs and reached for the first aid kit containing the pills Désiré had prepared for me. "Right here." I popped a tablet out of the foil packet and swallowed it with some water. My throat felt raw, and I tasted metal.

I rummaged through the bag and grabbed the packet of crisps and the envelope containing the photos. "Have you gone through them yet?" I asked.

"No; tell me what you see," he said, without moving his eyes from the road. He hunched over the steering wheel. I felt myself frown.

"Can't you see at night?"

That made him leer at me, his frown matching my own, and then he went back to concentrating on the road.

"I'm just tired, I guess. Stop staring at me and tell me what you see in the photos."

Maybe he didn't want anyone to know that his eyesight was going. He looked like he could be over forty. It didn't seem appropriate to ask him his age, though; yet one more reminder of the distance my memory loss had now put between us.

I glanced through all the photos first and then started organizing them. I put similar images together, but many of them were blurry—one looked like the close-up of an eye, while another focused only on lips. I took those and placed them at the back of the pack.

In total, there were fifteen or sixteen photos that I could make sense of. The weirdest of sensations ran through me as my eyes scanned each image; a sensation I fought desperately to conceal from Ralph. My eyes widened, and my hands began to shake. It was almost as if the photos were speaking to me, and suddenly I was able to recall things that I had no idea I knew. Each of the photos had resonance, and there was a familiarity about them that was somehow disorienting. In those moments when I looked through them for the first time, even though I was unable to remember even the most precious details of my own existence, I could recall information that was thousands of years old.

Each of the synapses in my brain were firing with minutiae of a civilization long since lost. Pressure built behind my eyes, and I decided that the only way to rid myself of it was to try and vocalize my thoughts. Fortunately for me, Ralph's eyes were still very much on the road, and so, by controlling the tone of my voice and speaking contemplatively, he had no idea of the extent to which I was affected by the images.

"Okay, most of the photos are too blurry to clearly make out what is going on, but they're definitely surveillance photos relating to the shipment we were following. The first three are of the shipyard; nothing out of the ordinary, just the yard, the container, and the container's reference number — '369182'. There are two snaps of the mummy of Amenemhat, one of which shows his whole body wrapped in linen bandages and molded plaster. From the looks of it, his sarcophagus was made from stone and painted with inscriptions on the inside. Also within is Amenemhat's mask in cartonnage—that's the mask that's molded onto his mummy and painted to look like an animal."

I stopped talking. It was strange I knew anything about this stuff.

Ralph raised his eyebrows in response; clearly some of the language I used was very topic-specific and hinted at the fact that I was starting to much more clearly grasp the situation that we were in. I thought he was going to say something, but he didn't, and so I looked at the next set of photos and carried on telling Ralph what I saw.

"There is one of Amenemhat's face, or rather the gold and black painted linen cloth covering him. And then there are five photos relating to the jewels you mentioned. There are three jewels, all emerald green in color and of various sizes, outlined in elegant gold. Lastly, there's three photos of some hieroglyphic markings on a stone tablet, but I don't know what these markings mean."

What I didn't say— mainly because I didn't understand how I knew all this—was that there were depictions of the Goddesses

Isis and Nephthys on Amenemhat's coffin. From what I could remember, legend spoke of them safeguarding the deceased in the afterlife.

There were also depictions of Apep, the Eater of souls, the embodiment of chaos who appeared as a giant serpent or crocodile. The other name by which he was known was Apophis, and he had lived in the underworld, waiting for Ra.

Ra; the deity of the sun. The creator of the sky, the earth and the underworld—the place where the sun sets and only the dead reside.

I seemed to remember reading books that claimed there were many battles between Apep and Ra. Some described Ra's victory, whereby he dismembered Apep and disposed of him, scattering his body parts in places that no one could find.

Now that I thought about it, it all reminded me of vampires and their preference for night over day. Was Apep, patiently awaiting Ra in the underworld, the master of all vampires? Was Ra Apep's ultimate destroyer? Did Ra chase Apep to sleep at dawn—was that why vampires were absent during the day? And did Apep collect his souls by feeding on his victims' blood?

I wasn't sure whether I should tell Ralph about this stuff I knew about Egyptian gods; about the soul eater and the creator. Something in the back of my mind—probably the same place as where the information came from—told me I sounded crazy.

Ralph said something, but I didn't make out the words. A car passed us at a snail's pace. I lifted the photos close to my face so that I could tell Ralph what else I saw, but that movement was s-l-o-w and blurry.

"Sorry, what did you say?" I said, mumbling.

"You're pale. What's wrong?"

"Nothing." My vision cleared and I noticed we had parked outside a house. "Is this Marcus's house?"

It looked like a nice enough neighborhood. Some houses were double stories, while others had the idyllic white picket fence. Marcus's house was a single story with brown shutters over the windows and white paint on the walls that had started to chip away to reveal a dull gray color. Only one light illuminated the inside of the house, and the porch light was on. Everything else drowned in darkness. I had to fight the urge to tell Ralph to keep driving.

I flinched when Ralph spoke. "Yeah, that's his," he said. "Marcus said he was home, but it looks awfully quiet." He undid his buckle and unlocked the car doors.

I needed to get a grip. Why was I so jumpy? There was blood still left in the I.V. There was no way I could crouch outside someone's home with a drip in my arm and a blood bag in my hand. I yanked the needle out, and blood sprayed all over my face and down the front of my shirt. I let go of the needle and pressed down on the wound.

"Jesus, Blaire! Couldn't you wait a goddam minute? Let me help you."

I felt the warm liquid drip down my cheeks and over my mouth and chin. I licked my lips and swallowed the warm blood, savoring the metallic taste, even swirling it around my mouth before swallowing it.

I removed my hand from the wound, brought it to my mouth and started sucking on the cut. I could feel my eyelids fluttering as I drank.

I enjoyed it. I wanted more.

It was not my doing.

Those were not my thoughts.

Where did they come from, and why could I hear them?

Confusion set in.

Ralph came around the car and opened my door. There was a

flash of panic in his eyes, but he didn't hesitate. He pushed me gently to one side and went for the first aid kit. He yanked it open, and the contents flew onto my lap and the floor near my feet. He grabbed a piece of gauze and softly pulled my arm away from my mouth.

I opened my mouth, but I couldn't think of anything to say, so I closed it again. Ralph applied pressure while, with one hand, he folded a piece of the gauze into a small square and placed it on the wound, grabbing my index finger to keep it in place for him. He removed a large plaster from the first aid kit and placed it atop the gauze, pressing it firmly into place.

Ralph pursed his lips as his cold blue eyes avoided mine. When he was done, he stepped away from the car—away from me—and waited for a few silent moments before he spoke. "Put everything in the bag. Time for us to see if Marcus is home."

He was angry.

Fifteen

I emptied the packet with the snacks and bottles of water out onto the carpet by my feet and unhooked the blood bag. I placed the drip and blood bag in the packet along with the bloody gauze and the plastic strip from the plaster and climbed out of the car. Without looking back at me, Ralph locked the car and walked in silence along the path toward Marcus's front door.

Ralph knocked, but there was no answer. I walked to the side of the house to see into the window that had a light on. I saw a sofa near the window, a dining room table and an open-plan kitchen. Eerily similar to both mine and Ralph's homes, like we had hired the same contractor to build our houses.

"Maybe he's in the basement? Don't we have keys to each other's homes?"

Ralph gave one stern nod, reached for his car keys again and found the key he was looking for. He slipped the key into the lock and opened the door.

A wave of warm air hit me in my face as I walked into the

lounge, and it smelt stuffy and stale with a hint of something bitter and rotten. My lip pulled upward.

"Marcus, are you home?" Ralph yelled into the empty house.

The longer we stayed inside the house, the hotter the house felt.

"Is his hidden door also under the fridge?" I whispered.

Again, Ralph nodded once and headed for the kitchen. He felt behind the fridge and hit the switch, and then the motor started, pulling the fridge away from the wall to reveal an opening in the floor.

With my left hand trailing along the wall for comfort, I descended the stairs, and just before I reached the bottom, the lights came on. Ralph moved away from the light switch and stairs in order to search the room. I followed closely behind him. When he stopped, I bumped into him. Ralph grunted. I backed away.

"Sorry," I said, with an edge of sarcasm. "I didn't mean to bump into you, and I didn't mean to... you know," — I couldn't say it, — "back there in the car. I don't know what happened." I shrugged.

The color of his eyes changed with his mood until they were no longer blue. They looked like storm clouds to me—and the storm was about to break.

"You need to figure out what is happening to you, Blaire. Maybe you do need to see that vamp and ask him what the fuck he did to you. Humans don't drink blood." His words were tainted with disgust. "Especially not our own."

I nodded, agreeing with him; I didn't understand why I drank the blood. I've never tasted my blood that way. Ever.

Ralph turned away from me and walked around the room. It was a room so similar to his and to mine that, at a glance, we could easily see that there was nothing out of place. I walked in the opposite direction toward the little make-shift kitchen where the table and fridge stood. Marcus's table also had silver containers for tea, coffee and sugar, but he didn't have a coffee machine—just a kettle. I opened the fridge, and it was packed full of food—enough to feed you comfortably for at least a month, if you rationed properly.

"He's not here," I said. "Nothing looks out of place. Let's go back upstairs. Maybe he left something lying around."

Without waiting for Ralph to answer, I climbed the stairs. When I reached the top of the opening and stepped out, the room downstairs went dark, and I heard him climbing back up.

In the main bedroom, the stench of something rotten brought tears to my eyes. I covered my nose and mouth with my hand, but that didn't work; the stink took my breath away, forcing me to take short, shallow breaths.

"God, what's that smell?" Ralph asked, towering behind me.

He pushed past and went into the en-suite bathroom while I checked the closets. There was nothing of interest in the room. By the time I finished, Ralph was still in the bathroom.

"What's taking you so long?" I stopped short in the door-jamb, dropped my hands to my sides and couldn't tear my eyes away from what I saw in the bathtub.

"Now I know why he didn't want us to come to his house," Ralph said, his voice filled with emotion.

I nodded, but he didn't see me; he, too, was staring at the contents of the bathtub. My eyes were slowly trying to adjust to what I was seeing. At first, it was blurry, but after blinking a few times, I started to roll the picture around in my mind until I focused on it again. And then, I couldn't unsee it.

I should be used to seeing sights like this. But apparently the new me was finding this disturbing.

The first thing I saw was a bone; the humerus of an arm,

sticking out from a mass of gray rotting meat enclosed in pale skin that was wrinkled from lying in the dark liquid for some time. It was apparent that the body had been dismembered and it was not there in its entirety. The femur moved, animated by the little things moving in and around it from where green puss leaked into the bathtub. I gagged and swallowed. The edges of the limbs were jagged, as though they had been hacked off by a saw or a blunt object—or, possibly, teeth. Someone was sick enough to leave the plug in, so that the liquid had pooled in the bathtub and surrounded all the limbs, creating the horrifying scene.

"It wasn't me, before you say it."

A voice from behind startled me. I jumped inside the bathroom, almost knocking Ralph over and into the bathtub. He was quick enough to stop me from falling into him and steadied my balance. I had a death grip on his left arm; everything was scaring me like my body was overly sensitive, and everything was freaking me the fuck out.

"I didn't do it." Marcus pleaded. He lifted his hands like he was praying. They were shaking, his cheeks were pink, and a thick layer of sweat beaded on his face. His shirt clung to his body, and his pupils were so large they were all I could see from where I was standing. There wasn't a hint of blue visible in those beady eyes.

Ralph let go of me and walked toward Marcus.

"What's going on with you, Marcus? Who's in your tub?" Ralph jabbed a finger into Marcus's chest.

"I told you, I was feeling ill. I'm sick—really sick." Marcus stepped backward until his legs caught against the bed and he fell onto it. Ralph moved to assist him, but Marcus waved him away. "It's just the tablets; were-animals have a fast-acting metabolism, so any antibiotics I take needs to be strong. The ones I'm on sometimes knock me for six."

"Do you think it's Shane?" Ralph pointed his thumb behind him in the direction of the tub.

"Yeah. I'd just found him when you called earlier, and I haven't had the stomach to move him."

"Since when are assassins squeamish?" I said in an accusatory tone. Who was I to throw stones—but I did, anyway. "And why didn't you tell Ralph about it?"

"I know how bad it looks." Marcus slumped his shoulders forward, looking defeated. "But trust me—I know nothing more about Shane's disappearance than you do. Whoever put him there is trying to frighten us."

Whoever had sent the message, we certainly received it.

As I watched him, the color ran from Marcus's face, and a faint tremor started in his hands. Maybe he was ill. If he was, he needed to see a better doctor.

"Who have you gone to for help?" I asked. "You look like shit."

"Gee, thanks." He winced and started to shake more visibly. "One of Désiré's people helped me when she couldn't, but I think I need to go back and get something different." Sweat poured down his forehead, and he stood. "I have to go."

He darted out of his bedroom, and I heard the front door slam shut before I could protest. He might be ill, but he was still damn fast.

I turned to Ralph, who was giving me a deadpan look, but his eyes gave something away; even he felt a little out of his depth.

"Now what?" I asked, starting to fidget with the plaster on my left arm; it was itching. The more I rubbed the plaster, the more it itched. I pulled the plaster off, and black stuff oozed out of the wound. "Ew," I said when I saw it.

"Let me see." Ralph took my arm and lifted it up to his face. "That black stuff is killing you, Blaire. You need to see that vampire. Now."

I started to shake my head in protest, but Ralph was persistent.

"I don't think we have enough time to figure out who attacked you and get this curse removed," he said. "We need to act now." The look he gave me spoke only of fear.

"Okay. Fine." I took my arm away from him to look at the poison pulsing from my wound. It was time to accept that no amount of pills could combat it. "Let's go see the vampire."

Sixteen

It was after midnight when we arrived at Léon's house. In truth, it was less a house and more a converted warehouse. It took up an entire block; a huge double story warehouse with rooms and walls that kept moving. Who devised his security for him? It was an awesome idea.

Ralph parked near one of the first doors we came across. It was in the same street as the alley, and something hardened in my stomach.

I stared at the cars parked in front of us, and when I looked up, something floated through the air, smashed through the windscreen and jumped on me while something else hit me from the left-hand side and bit down.

I jerked in the chair, hitting my head against the window and making an '*Ah*' sound loud enough to give Ralph a fright. I felt the car rock from the movement.

"What was that?" Ralph asked while unbuckling.

"There were two of them, Ralph. There were two were-animals who attacked me. Not one—but two of them. The one who bit my left side was a were-wolf, and the other who tore through my left thigh—he was a were-lion."

The flashback was clear. I remembered watching them as they had jumped over the wall of the dark alley from the park and landed on me at the same time. There were teeth, claws and loud noises, and they had been too fast for me. Too quick for me to reach for my gun. They had removed the gun first, knowing I would have silver bullets locked and loaded. They sliced through the leather strap of my gun holster, sending the gun flying. The impact of them landing on me at the same time had been so severe that I hit my head on the concrete and cracked my skull. I had heard that crunching sound as the bone fractured. And then I had lost consciousness for a few seconds, and in effect, lost time along with the rest of my memory. But something or someone else had stopped them or frightened them because they had jumped over that wall as quickly as they came and left me there to bleed to death.

My door opened, and Ralph was beside me. I didn't see him move. He was waving his hand in front of my face, asking me something, but all I saw was his moving lips; I couldn't hear what he was saying.

Something tore through my body and down my left arm, and I screamed. I heard that. I closed my eyes and concentrated on my breathing as I struggled for air. I needed to calm down.

When I opened my eyes, a gray blur clouded my vision and something big was headed our way. I wanted to warn Ralph, but my arms were lead, and my mouth too dry to say anything. The gray blur pushed Ralph out of the way and picked me up.

I was in someone's arms, and we were running. Fast. I tried to see if Ralph was near, but the gray cloud was still around me, the murky blanket blocking my vision.

After everything I had gone through within a week, I was

tough and seemed to handle a lot. But now that my eyesight was going, I was afraid. I thought of the black stuff inside me and how it was tearing through my veins, eating its way through me while I was still alive. I was afraid that maybe, just maybe, I would die for real, vampire mark or not.

I heard panicked voices, people running around, and the wheels of beds being moved. The person holding me, laid me gently on top of a bed, and I sank into the mattress. I felt my bones give way, and I melted into the soft cushion below.

There was another gray figure hovering over me, trying to look into my eyes with a light, but my eyes could not clearly make them out. My eyes were no longer mine. There was frantic shouting, and someone lifted my left arm to look at the wound. I heard them rip off the new plaster we had put over it—and nothing after that.

T he beep of a monitor mirroring my heartbeat told me I wasn't dead. By some miracle, someone had saved me—again. I hoped this was the last time anyone needed to.

I smelled antiseptic spray and tasted it in my mouth. I moved, and someone asked if I was awake; if I was okay.

I wiggled my toes, and they moved. My knees were next, and then I could flex my fingers and make a fist, but when I tried to lift my hands, I couldn't. That made me open my eyes and stare down at the restraints keeping my hands in place.

"You kept pulling on the drip, so we had to restrain you." I couldn't focus on his face, but I knew the voice. Sebastian came closer and started loosening the restraints. "I'm glad you're awake. How do you feel?"

"Not dead." I tried for a joke, but nobody laughed, not even me. It wasn't really that funny, but almost dying three times in one week was starting to sound a lot like '*the boy who cried wolf*'.

When my hands were free, I rubbed my wrists and found that my eyes could now focus—that gray blur had gone. I saw Sebastian clearly, and while I focused on him, I saw something moving out of the corner of my eye. Ralph sat up in the chair he had been lying on.

"Hey, you. Welcome back to the land of the living."

That made me smile—his jokes were funnier than mine.

"At least one of us is getting some beauty sleep," I said.

Ralph stood to my right, smiling, but the smile didn't reach his eyes.

"What's wrong? The look on both of your faces is scaring me." My heart skipped a beat, and it suddenly felt like it had dropped to my stomach. Something else must have happened while I had been out of it.

Ralph looked at Sebastian, and then they burst out laughing. That made me smile; the asshole's were messing with me.

"Glad the two of you are getting along."

"I'm sorry, Blaire; I couldn't resist." Ralph patted my right hand and held it, squeezed it for a second then let go. "You are going to be just fine. The curse is gone." He looked at Sebastian again, moving his head slightly as if to tell him to finish the story.

"Once Ralph explained some of your symptoms, we realized what happened to you—and who did it," Sebastian added.

I raised my eyebrows. "Really? Care to share?"

Sebastian held his breath and exhaled slowly. "It was one of the were-lions. He cheated on his girlfriend, which is never a smart move when she happens to be a witch. When she found out about it, she cursed him in the hope that whoever he was sleeping with would die. When he bit you and clawed your thigh, he passed on the curse to you, and you became infected with whatever that black stuff was."

"Who was it, Sebastian? I have to know who did this to me."

I needed to put a name to the animal I'd seen in my vision; in my memory.

Sebastian wouldn't look me in the eyes. "We have handled it, Blaire." He glanced at me as he said my name. His face was stone-cold, completely devoid of emotion.

"Dammit—tell me, Sebastian! I don't care how you handle it. I still need to know who cut me up and left me to die."

"It was Danny."

"Who's Danny?" I furrowed my brows.

"Danny is Miles's brother."

I wanted to ask who Miles was, but then I remembered; Miles was the were-wolf who was on Léon's security detail—he had been accompanying Léon and Sebastian when they found me after the attack.

"But there were two of them, Sebastian. It wasn't only Danny."

Sebastian frowned. "Danny said it was only him."

"Well, he's lying. There were two of them. My memory is slowly returning, and I remember two of them jumping over the wall that separates the alley from the park and attacking me. Two of them." I lifted my index and middle fingers to reinforce the point.

"How do you even know it was Danny?" I asked, trying to relax against the pillow.

"Miles brought Danny to us for help, and his girlfriend, Seraphine, was with them. Danny had black stuff coming out of his mouth—the very same black stuff coursing through your veins—and when he thought he was going to die, he confessed to Seraphine and begged for her forgiveness. Seraphine admitted to cursing him and, therefore, anyone he made love to, bit or scratched."

Sebastian cleared his throat, pulled up a chair and sat down. "Mel asked Danny if he had bitten anyone, and he couldn't answer her—or rather, he chose not to. The second time Mel stitched you together, she noticed your blood wasn't as red as it should be, but she didn't really think of it again. Not until Danny came in. That's when she called me and told me what she thought. At first, Seraphine refused to lift the curse because she wanted Danny to suffer. Then, when you arrived two hours later, we brought in Seraphine so she could see the damage she had caused, and she immediately removed the curse. Mel put you on a drip, and that's when you started to come around. Fortunately, there is no permanent damage, and Seraphine has asked if she can come by a bit later to apologize to you."

"What else did Danny say?"

"Danny told me he had been hired to kill you, but also that he acted alone."

"Who hired him to kill me? Have you been able to find out why?"

"He didn't want to say."

I raised an eyebrow. I didn't believe Danny had acted alone. "He's lying, Sebastian," I said. "Is Danny still alive? I want to talk to him myself."

"He is, but you can't talk to him now. He is," — Sebastian waved a hand in the air while trying to think of the right word, — "as you would say, being held prisoner and punished for what he's done."

"I don't care what you do or who you talk to get this done, but I need to speak with him. Tonight."

"Not tonight, Blaire—please, not tonight," he pleaded, and his cold eyes softened, the tension in his shoulders easing as he sat back. "There's no way you're strong enough to have that conversation tonight." I couldn't decide whether he looked defeated or just tired.

"If not tonight, then when?"

I didn't know what was going on, but I let it go, for now. I still wanted to talk to Danny, but Sebastian did have a point. I felt as though I had been hit by a bus, and any sort of confrontation was likely to push me past breaking point.

"Soon, I promise." Sebastian stood and started walking toward the door but stopped near my feet. He touched my left foot over the bedding and said, "Both of you need to stay here. No walking around. Léon is hosting some guests from out-of-town, and he'd rather you didn't meet them."

"Why?" I asked. "Why can't we meet these mystery people?"

"They are vampires, and you are an assassin, Blaire. Not a good mix."

I couldn't argue with that, but it did leave me wondering why they might be afraid of an assassin with no cause to harm them.

When I didn't respond, he added, "Please don't leave this room. I will come back later with Seraphine." And then he left, closing the door softly behind him.

My head was spinning as I tried to make sense of the latest developments. Our target had been Léon, and the man protecting him was related to the man who had been paid to target me. Was that why I couldn't speak to Danny—because he was Miles's brother?

"That was a bit intense." Ralph broke the silence. He reached for my hand and held it. I wasn't entirely sure whether it was intended to comfort me or him, but the tension in his shoulders seemed to disappear completely just by touching my hand and his breathing wasn't as fast. Even the frown between his eyes were gone. "How are you really feeling?"

"Much better." I squeezed his hand. "You seem calmer, too."

"Yeah, I think that witch did something to me."

"What did she do?" I sat up, waiting for my head to whoosh, but it didn't.

Whenever there was a witch involved, things always seemed to turn to shit, so when Ralph said she had done something to him, that made me pay attention.

"It's nothing bad, I promise. When she saw how stressed I was over your condition, she touched my arm and said I would feel better after you woke. I didn't feel anything when she touched me, but the skin beneath her touch became warm." His index finger traced along his arm to the place where, I assumed, she had touched him.

I touched the area beside his finger and found that it was unusually warm. "Are you sure you're okay?" I asked, studying his face for any indication of discomfort, but nothing about his expression suggested he was suffering in any way.

He grinned. "Are you worried about little old me?" he teased, sitting on the sofa.

I tilted my head to the side and pouted.

Seventeen

C omfortable silence filled the air. Ralph was reading a
magazine to pass the time, and I could finally think
more clearly. My first thought was of the realization
that I was naked beneath the covers. I needed to find my clothes
and get dressed.

"Um, where are my clothes?" I asked.

Ralph glanced up from the magazine. "They had to cut your
clothes from you when we were brought in, but Sebastian came
by earlier to drop off a few items." He went to a door on the far
left of the room and opened it. Beyond the door was a tiny closet
with several items of clothing hanging within.

I was about to get up when the drip in my arm caught on the
bedding. There was no way I could get dressed with an I.V. in
my arm.

"Is there any underwear you can give me, please?"

His smile widened. "There are at least three black pairs of
matching panties and bras for you to choose from." He raised an

161

eyebrow. "Do you need any help climbing into them?" he said flirtatiously.

"No, thank you. Just bring any." I sounded angry.

Ralph handed me a set, and I lifted the covers well above my shoulders so that only my head could be seen while I pulled on the panties with my free hand. I slipped my right arm through the right strap of the bra before I realized that I couldn't put it on because of the drip.

Ralph laughed.

"What's so funny?"

"Let me help you." He came around to the side of the bed and looked at the drip. "It's almost empty. Do you just want to remove it?"

I nodded.

He started pulling the plaster that kept the needle in place when the door opened. A woman entered first. She had the longest chestnut-colored hair I'd ever seen, reaching down almost to her knees. She was a similar height to me because her head was also level with Sebastian's shoulder. He entered right behind her and closed the door. She was curvy in all the right places and wore a loose-fitting floral dress with thin straps. Her oval face was pale, and her lips and nose were thin. Her brown hair and eyebrows made her eyes appear the lightest green I had ever seen, so much so that they were translucent. She was exquisite and exotic-looking. She took my hand in both of hers.

"I'm Seraphine and I'm sorry for the pain I caused you. Please accept my humble apology," she said with a slight accent. Still holding my hand, she curtsied and bowed her head.

Her hands felt warm in mine. When they started to get hot, I tried to free my hand from her grip as gently as possible. How could I tell a woman to leave my hand alone when she could kill me with a single snap of her fingers?

I smiled. "Thank you for apologizing, but you couldn't control what Danny did. I'm sorry he hurt you; he drove you to do what you thought was best at the time." There, that sounded good enough for me.

She let go of my hand, and her arms fell to her sides. Her haunting eyes pierced mine as if they were trying to peek inside my soul. I glanced nervously at Sebastian, but all he did was shrug.

"Thank you for accepting my apology, Blaire. I am in your debt."

With her hypnotic eyes boring inside me—through me—I couldn't look away. My breathing became labored, and heat swam around me, burning my skin. I wanted nothing more than to get away from her.

"Seraphine, what are you doing?" That was Sebastian's voice. I couldn't look at him; all I saw was endless green as her eyes remained fixed on mine. "Seraphine?" Sebastian's voice sounded strained.

Suddenly, I could breathe again, and I swam out from the water of her mind to fill my lungs with air. I climbed out from the hot pool she had placed me in and walked to the shore where the wind began to cool me down.

Seraphine blinked and broke the metaphysical link. "She is different, Sebastian. I have met no one who can do this—especially not a human. And yet, here she is, right in front of me."

The seriousness her face had shown when she first entered the room was gone, replaced now with wonderment. Her skin glowed, her eyes lit up and her smile was wide.

I didn't understand why she needed to display her power that way; like she was testing me.

Sebastian fell silent. He had his habitual blank face on. The man was so hard to read.

"Why did you do that, Seraphine?" I asked, clearing my throat. "It felt like you were trying to suffocate me."

"I'm sorry, dear, but there was something in your aura when I first entered that made me curious."

"My aura?"

She nodded. "Yes. At first, it was weak, but after I lifted the curse, it brightened. I've never seen one so bright—so white —before."

"What does that mean? You're the second person to tell me that."

"Sebastian told me you have no memory of your life before the attack." Her expression solemn as she spoke. "Because your aura is pure, Blaire, I had to see who you are."

"What does that mean?"

"It means you have a direct link to the spiritual world; you are open and receptive to the divine world, to my world—to *any* world. And with this gift, you can borrow powers from others, store them and use them when you need to. You can almost be" —she paused, thinking of the correct word to use— "lethal."

My mouth gaped open.

"Was she born with this link, or is it as a result of the attack?" Ralph asked.

"Oh no, she was born with this." Seraphine seemed sure of this.

I felt my eyes widen. Had I known this before the attack but had chosen to keep it a secret from everyone? Even Ralph seemed not to know about it. Shit. Something deep down in the pit of my stomach clenched tightly—and I knew.

I knew that no one was meant to know this about me. There was a reason I had kept it from everyone. Now my secret was out, it could only spell trouble.

"Is she in danger?" Ralph said what I was thinking.

Seraphine and Sebastian exchanged a knowing glance that made my stomach twist. I believed in always trusting your gut instinct, and mine was waving red flags. Deep shit. I was in big trouble.

"It is possible," Seraphine answered and stepped back. "Again, I apologize for the intrusion of your mind. I didn't hurt you, did I?"

"No, you didn't, but you've given me a shitload to think about. What must I do with this information, Seraphine? How can I understand more of it?" I sounded angry again. I guessed that I could ask Désiré to help me by looking into her coven's literature, but I did not know how long that would take, and, besides, she didn't seem to know all that much when she mentioned my aura. Perhaps Seraphine was the best chance I had of shedding some light on my abilities.

"Let me speak with my high priestess and await my return." She curtsied again and started for the door. She whispered something in Sebastian's ear and then left.

"What? What did she say to you?" I asked. My anger flared, and I crossed my arms over the covers, the bra strap still hanging loosely from my right arm.

"She said I must keep you here, where you're safe. I said I would try."

"I've had enough bad shit happen to me the last couple of days to last a lifetime. What I want is to get out of this bed, get dressed, and do something. I need to find out what is happening to me and why I was attacked in the first place. Someone paid to have me killed. Do you understand that, Sebastian?"

"Let me get Mel to help you," Sebastian said, opening the door to leave, and it clicked once he had closed it.

"Did he just lock the fucking door?"

"Geez, Blaire, tone down the language. You cuss, but not normally this much."

"Well, I guess no one really knows what I'm like, now do they, Ralph?"

Ralph turned hurtful eyes on me and fell silent. He stood against the wall, staring at me as though I had sprouted a second head.

I didn't have a watch, but minutes went by and an uncomfortable silence hung in the air. Ralph rested his head against the wall, his arms crossed over his broad chest, his left leg bent, and his foot pressed against the wall. He avoided eye contact—it looked like he was counting the tiny holes in the ceiling. I removed the bra strap from my right arm; I felt silly with it only half-on. Mel was on her way to remove the drip, and then I would dress properly.

The lock clicked, and the door opened. A woman I presumed to be Mel stepped through with Sebastian just behind her. She was slim and had platinum-colored hair that stopped at her shoulders. Something in the way she carried herself reminded me of Sebastian, and I began to assume she was most likely a were-animal, too. I envied her hair color and wondered whether her fur was the same color when she assumed her animal-form. Like Seraphine and myself, she, too, came up to Sebastian's shoulders.

Her eyes seemed to smile when her lips did, and the anger I was holding onto so tightly began to dissolve. My jaw ached from the clenching. She glided over to me and started removing things. When she pulled on the needle to remove it, I focused on a spot on the wall.

In the blink of an eye, Sebastian moved from the doorjamb to stand next to me. I hated when were-animals did that—moving too fast for my brain to register. His eyes flickered from me to

Ralph and back to me. "Did you two have a fight?" he asked, his face close to mine.

"That's none of your business," I said with a sarcastic smile, and my anger flared again.

I felt a prick on my left hand, and a small yelping sound escaped my lips. Mel placed a cotton ball over the hole and pressed firmly to stop the bleeding. As quickly as it came, my anger dissolved.

"Okay, boys; out," Mel said, and the two men left. She grabbed jeans, a t-shirt, and a pair of shoes and socks from the closet. She left the shoes on the floor near to me and placed the clothing on the bed.

"Why are you so angry?" she asked.

"I don't know." I lay my head back on the pillow, my right hand cradling my left.

She touched my left arm, and the anger started to fade again.

"How can you calm me down with just your touch?"

"I'm a were-wolf, dear. That's one of the things I can do. It helps with my real job," she said, winking.

"Can't I hold your hand forever?"

Mel laughed. "No, I have a day job."

"Can you teach me? The soothing touch, I mean?"

She considered that for a moment and said, "I can try to help you, if you like?"

"I would. When things settle down, I would like that very much."

"I'll give you my number. Call me when you're ready." She wrote her number on a piece of paper and placed it on top of the pile of clothing.

"Thank you."

"Are any of your memories coming back yet?"

"Not really." I shrugged.

She made a 'hmm' sound and reached for the bra.

"Thanks, but I can dress myself." I started slipping my arms through the bra straps, fixed my breasts in place, and fastened the back. I grabbed the shirt and pulled it on, threw the covers back and pulled the jeans on. I sat back on the bed and pulled on the socks and shoes.

"Are there any toiletries for me to use?"

"Try the bathroom." She gestured with her right arm toward the bathroom door. It was the door to the left of the closet. Once inside, I locked the door behind me.

I stared at my reflection in the mirror. My green eyes were the complete opposite of Seraphine's; mine were gray/blue instead of green, with a dark ring around the iris. There were dark shadows around my eyes, and my cheeks looked gaunt. I washed and dried my face, removing a layer of sweat. I applied deodorant that I found in the little bag on the basin along with a toothbrush and toothpaste, and brushed my teeth.

I felt better, but what I really wanted was a long, hot bath. With my hair in need of a good wash, I found an elastic and tied it back.

I heard talking from the other room and decided I didn't want to go back out there, but I had to. I inhaled and exhaled, unlocked the door and went back into the room where everyone was whispering.

Eighteen

I felt better now that I was dressed. Now, I needed a plan. We—Ralph and I—could check out the shipyard for any clues we might have missed first time around.

When I opened the bathroom door, the room fell silent as everyone turned to stare at me. There were two more people in the room, now—Léon and Roland, the vampiric star attraction from the club.

Léon's short hair was styled back with a few loose strands falling over his dark ocean-blue-colored eyes. He wore a gray long-sleeve vintage mandarin collar shirt with gold patterns laced everywhere, tight black pants and polished boots. I couldn't make out if the pants were leather, cotton or vinyl, as there was no shine to them—but they were tight, almost as though they had been painted on.

Léon came toward me with both hands out. "Blaire, so glad to see you up and about. You scared me."

I scared him? That was an interesting choice of words. We had only known each other for less than a week, and he used 'me' instead of 'us'—which was a generalization. Maybe I scared him, but only because of the mark we shared. Had he felt anything as I lay dying?

He held my hands in his and came closer than before. His lips brushed my cheek gently, and it tickled, sending shivers down my spine and raising the hairs all over my body.

"Did any of what was happening to me affect you?" I said near his ear.

He was still close to my face. "No, luckily, it did not," he said in a whisper. He let go of my hands. "I would have come sooner, but we have guests that needed my urgent attention. I believe Mel and Sebastian have treated you well?"

"Yes, thank you."

"This is Roland. I believe you saw him at the club the other night."

I felt heat creep up my neck as I began thinking about how his velvet voice reached those forbidden areas without touching me.

Léon continued. "We were on our way back to our guests when we decided to stop by before you leave."

Roland's shiny brown hair came up to his shoulders and seemed to shimmer in the light like a life-force all of its own. He was six feet tall, maybe, with deep-set brown eyes and a square jaw. He wore a tailored white dress shirt that curved to his body, diamond cufflinks, no tie, black slacks, and black boots.

Roland stepped forward with an open hand. I gave him mine; his grip around my hand was firm yet delicate, and he brought it to his mouth and kissed my knuckles. The sensation from the kiss was both tender and electrifying all at once. I guess he had centuries to practice his flirtatious moves.

When he brought my hand back down, I glanced at his hand and noticed a scar; it looked like a burn.

He noticed me staring and opened his hand so that I could see all of it. "It was priests," he said sadly. "They burned my body with crosses."

I didn't know what to say; he was old, and the scars had been with him for years. I didn't think saying 'I'm sorry' to someone like him would matter anymore.

Instead, I said, "What happened to the priests?"

The corners of his mouth tilted upward. "I killed them naturally." He let go of my hand.

Of course, he killed them. You couldn't burn a vampire with a cross and expect to live a fruitful life.

"I thought vampires could heal?"

"Not from holy water or the burn of a cross, I'm afraid. I will live with this until I am eventually staked through the heart."

Both vampires started laughing. Roland's laugh was smooth and velvety—the kind of laugh that could make one wish for him to do naughty things to you—while Léon's was deep and crisp. There was nothing more spectacular than listening to the laughs of these two vampires, as they were usually serious, ruthless and moody creatures of the night. Sebastian laughed with them—a mixture of a purr and a low growl and deeper than Léon's, it was very much the sound I expected from a wereleopard.

Mel was quiet, her expression serious, and I wondered if she even liked Roland.

Ralph and I watched the men laughing. Once the laughter had died down, the two vampires walked toward the door.

I had so many questions for the two of them that I couldn't let them leave yet. "And what about your palms?" I asked Roland. "Did you grab hold of the crosses when they attacked you?" When Roland had offered his hand to me, there had been marks visible all over his palm which didn't look as old as the burn on its reverse.

Roland balled his hands into fists, and pink lines formed across the pale skin of his knuckles—he must have fed very well after he woke for the evening to show that much pink.

"That happened a couple of days ago. It was an accident." His reply was curt.

"I didn't know this. Did it happen at the club?" Léon asked, wanting to look at Roland's hands, but Roland pulled away from his master.

"It's nothing, Léon." Roland held his hands behind his back.

"Why is this the first I'm hearing of such an accident, and at one of my clubs? An accident which could scar a vampire, Roland?" Léon's voice was stern, and power rolled from him and into the other vampire.

Roland lifted his head to look at Léon and held his hands out in front of him, palms up. Both hands were heavily scarred, as though he had held onto something hot for too long.

"I was clumsy. One patron at the club threw a bottle with holy water at me, and I caught it. It spilled and burned my hands. I did not come to you with this because you have enough to worry about and I've taken care of it." Roland bowed his head and clasped his hands behind his back again.

"Very well, but do not make the mistake of thinking you know what is best for me or my club, Roland. This is your last warning."

"Yes, Léon."

Léon turned to us with his hand on the door handle and said to me, "You and I need to talk about a few things. Will you come back in a day or two?"

I wanted to talk to him now about the fact that we had been hired to kill him. I glanced at Ralph and tried to talk with my eyes, but I didn't know if he knew me well enough to under-stand what I was asking.

"Uh, okay, sure, I can come back. But there is something we need to ask you now, if you don't mind." The tone I used made clear that I wasn't giving him the option.

"What?" The word was filled with anger. But I surmised he was upset with Roland and not with me.

I hoped his reaction wouldn't be as harsh once he found out what I wanted to say.

Ralph realized what I wanted to ask and gave me the A-Okay by tilting his head—we needed to tell Léon about the contract on his life and to question him about the missing mummy and the jewels.

"We know about the missing mummy of Amenemhat, and the jewels," I blurted.

Léon's body stiffened, but his face held no expression. He tried to block his emotions, but it was too late; I already saw his discomfort.

"And what is it you think you know?"

"To be honest, I wasn't sure when would be the best time to raise this, but our company, Ulysses Assassins, was given the contract to kill you, Léon. From what we found out, it's all because of the jewels hidden with the mummy you shipped over from Egypt. The same shipment that mysteriously disap-peared the evening I was attacked."

Roland started fidgeting with his left cufflink while Léon let go of the door handle and faced me.

"Is the contract still valid?"

"No," — I glanced at Ralph, and he nodded his agreement, — "when someone tried to kill me and you saved my life, our priorities sort of changed. Whoever attacked me also killed a friend of ours, Shane—the torso Sebastian and I found in my car.

We need to find his killer. You need to find Amenemhat and the jewels. And we think it is the same person who did both."

A knowing look passed between Sebastian, Léon and Roland. It was Sebastian who spoke. "We had heard that Léon's life may be in danger. That is why he tripled his security and his schedule changes so often."

"Did you know we had been hired to kill you?" I looked at Léon. It was a good question. Why didn't I think of it before? Perhaps it had been the black stuff that was killing me from the inside. Now that I was rid of the infection, my brain seemed to work just fine; except my past, I still couldn't remember that.

"No, I didn't know who you were when we picked you off the cement in the alley." His voice sounded dry and sarcastic.

"We didn't know, Blaire." Sebastian echoed Léon, but his words were calmer and sincere.

"And what about Amenemhat?"

"We have been trying to locate the container and its contents. We inserted a tracker inside the sarcophagus before it left Egypt, but the signal seems scrambled and we can't locate it. We get a blip, and then it disappears again."

"Can you tell me the significance of Amenemhat?"

"We have no interest in Amenemhat; it is the jewels that are of great value, Blaire. They are priceless to a vampire."

"Go on."

Léon stepped closer, but Sebastian held a hand out to stop him from coming too close. Was it for Léon's safety—or mine? I frowned at Sebastian. Léon stood still, his arms straight against his sides.

"Do you know anything about Egyptology?"

"Strangely enough, I seem to remember quite a bit lately, but jog my memory and explain."

Ralph stood closer to the bed, so that if I needed him, he

could jump over and help. With everyone blocking his path, over the bed was the easiest. It's what I would have done.

"Stories are told of Apep, the god of darkness, who created men just like him by infecting them with his bite. Apep caused so much chaos in the underworld that he needed to be stopped. His nemesis was Ra, the god of light who created the earth, the sky and the underworld. Every time Ra visited the underworld, he and Apep would fight. Eventually, Ra decided upon the creation of three jewels of immense power, with which he hoped to destroy Apep.

"Centuries later, as the vampire population increased, some fed on powerful Egyptians. To stop the vampires, the Pharoahs had their scribes scour the scriptures until they came across the story of Ra's creation, and they realized that these three jewels harnessed the power to control the vampires—or kill them. It would strip vampires of their powers and leave them at the mercy of the one who held the jewels—but all three jewels had to be held together for their power to be unleashed.

"As my powers have grown, I have had many people try to destroy me. As you can see, all have failed, but I have heard of others searching for these jewels to use against me—to get me to obey. This I cannot allow, and so I found them first and had them brought here. But, somehow, someone knew and sought to steal them from me."

I let that sink in; I knew about the story of Apep and Ra, but I'd never heard mention of the jewels that could control vampires. If the government found out, they could use it as a weapon to control them all. A weapon that people would kill for; a weapon that would become very dangerous in the wrong hands.

"I don't recall any books documenting these jewels. Does the government know about them?"

"No, I don't think so, and it's not the government who have taken them. They would have used better resources to find the jewels, and they would have used them against my kind already. Which is not the case, as I still have all my powers." He raised his hands in front of him for me to see, as if to symbolize that there had been no change in him.

Point taken.

"So, do you think it's a vampire who took them from you? It would make sense. The reason as to why the jewels haven't been used yet—because doing so would stop their own powers."

"Precisely. No vampire—no sane vampire, that is—could use the jewels himself. The jewels would render the vampire mortal. It would have to be a human, or even a were-animal, who could use them, but we don't know for sure. I wanted to bring the jewels here for testing in a controlled environment."

I considered what Léon had told me for a moment. Having been in his care and seen firsthand how he conducted himself, I believed that what he said was true.

"We will help you find these jewels," I said, "but I also want the person responsible for attacking me and killing Shane. Can we help each other?" It was a fair trade, in my eyes.

"Sebastian can tell you all we know. He will go with you, but I need to stay here—we have out-of-town guests, and they must know none of this." Léon reached for the door again and opened it. "Thank you, Blaire. You too, Ralph."

The two vampires left. The rest of us remained silent.

"Shit." The sound of my voice eventually pierced the quiet.

Mel headed for the door. "Right then. I need to get out of here before the proverbial shit hits the fan. Sebastian, I'm going home. Call me when I'm needed."

"Thanks, Mel," Sebastian said. Turning to us, he said, "We have to go now before the security walls change and the vampires need to retire. The sun will be up in a couple of hours, and we have to be out of here."

Mel left first, but where she turned left, the three of us went right, with Sebastian leading us out of the maze. Eventually we exited the building without bumping into any vampires, but the door we were left standing near was nowhere near Ralph's car, which was parked on the far side of the building. We had to walk around the block to get there.

It was still dark, but the silver sliver of dawn was piercing its way through the night sky, and I shivered—not from the cold, but from thinking too hard about everything. We all agreed that we would go to the shipyard one last time, but at least this time around, we had keys to the office and Sebastian would help us in any way he could.

Léon was his brother—half-brother—and, despite Léon being a vampire, Sebastian loved him enough not to let him die or have any harm come to him. Despite being stronger than Léon because he was a were-leopard, he allowed his older brother to hold the throne. As long as his brother was Master of the City, he would stay the second-in-command.

Nineteen

One question still burned within me. Had Sebastian known that Ulysses had been hired to kill Léon and had me attacked to make sure I couldn't finish the job?

I stared at the back of Sebastian's head; he sat in the front seat as Ralph drove us to the shipyard. After everything Sebastian had done for me, could I bring myself to kill him if needed? I was supposed to be an assassin, after all—but since the attack, that life no longer meant anything to me. If Sebastian answered truthfully that he had been behind the attack, I didn't know if I could grab Ralph's gun and shoot him.

Sebastian must have felt my stare because he turned around, twisting his body in the front seat as far as the seat belt would allow.

I glared at him.

"What's wrong?" he said.

"Was it you?"

"Was what me?"

"Was it you who had me attacked?"

His eyes went big, their green coloring paling against the white, his mouth parting slightly. He shook his head. "No, I did not. I swear." His expression softened. "I want to know who is behind all this just as much as you do. We have compromised people working for us, and I need to know who they are, so we can be rid of them."

I relaxed slightly. There was a breach somewhere, and I felt reassured by his reaction that it wasn't Sebastian. He was right; they needed to flush the culprit out. This person knew about the shipment and when to steal it, and they achieved this right under their noses. Could Léon not tell when someone lied to his face? Could he not sense the guilt? Unless whoever was responsible was powerful enough to mask it.

"Who do you know that could use their power to conceal their involvement?"

Sebastian considered this for a moment. "Few," he said. "Roland and Jean-René are as old as Léon, but they are nowhere near as powerful. Charlotte is powerful, but she loves Léon. She would do anything to protect him; she would do nothing like this."

"What about those two from the club? Ian and Esther?"

"No, never. We would know if it was them."

"Any were-animal Léon is attached to or that he loved and hurt?"

That made Sebastian grin. "No, Léon just likes their blood. He isn't attached to any of them."

I didn't know why he was grinning at me.

"Besides the latest vamps, did anyone else arrive in the last two weeks or month that you think could be culpable?"

"No, there's been no other arrivals that I know of. And the vampire guests only arrived today, or rather last night."

The car stopped with a jolt, and I almost slammed into Sebastian's head.

"Geez, Ralph! What's with the stop?"

"Look, there are people there and I don't know if they would allow us to go any farther without being riddled with bullet holes."

Sebastian turned around in the front seat to look at our surroundings, and so did I. The shipyard was ahead of us, and between us and its perimeter fence were men dressed in black, all armed with machine guns and pointing them at us.

"Stay here," Sebastian said, climbing out of the car with his hands up. He walked to the front of the gate and spoke to the guards.

Sebastian motioned for us to come forward, so Ralph drove on and stopped right in front of the boom gate. All the guns were pointing to the sky, and Sebastian was laughing with one of the guards. My shoulders relaxed, and the knot in my stomach eased. I would live another day.

We climbed out of the car and joined Sebastian, and the three of us walked the rest of the way into the shipyard with four guards at our backs. Their presence was making me nervous, but at least their guns weren't pointing at us anymore. Just knowing that we needed so many guards made me realize that there were people out there who wanted us dead. I wished my memory would return so I could, once again, be the big bad assassin I was supposed to be.

I still didn't want to touch a gun, though.

We entered the first office. Sebastian explained that this was where Gaspard and Edgar kept the records. We started going through all the cabinets and folders when I remembered the container number from the photo— '369182'. I reached into my back pocket and pulled out the envelope that had been hidden between my mattress and the base of the bed. As I unfolded the envelope, I once more read the name of Léon's shipping company, 'F.C. *Armateurs*', written on it. I realized that we had never looked inside the envelope, but I did now and pulled out a piece of paper. On it was an address, and it was written in what seemed to be my handwriting.

I asked Sebastian for the address of the shipping company, and he gave it to me, but it didn't match the one on the paper. There was a map on one wall of Sterling Meadow, and I went to it and traced my finger across the map, searching for the address from the paper. There were a few addresses marked on the map, but none of them looked familiar. Both men came to stand on either side of me to see what I was doing.

"It was inside the envelope I found at my house, Ralph. None of us saw it."

Ralph took the note and helped me searching for the address on the map.

"What's the address?" Sebastian asked. Ralph handed him the note. "I know where this is."

Ralph and I turned to him at the same time.

Sebastian had paled, still staring at the note. "It's one of Léon's warehouses. It's a depository for storing priceless items. Only a handful of people know of its location."

When Sebastian showed us where it was on the map, it was not one of the addresses that had been circled.

"But because this warehouse is secret, there is no red circle," I stated.

"Exactly. Only a handful of us know about it."

"That narrows down the suspects."

"What do the circles mean?"

"It's all of Léon's properties."

"All of them?"

"Yes, all of them; he has quite the portfolio."

I guess you can't be a vampire and not gain businesses throughout the years, but there were over fifty circles dotted across the large map.

"How far are we from the warehouse?"

"It's about a twenty-to-thirty-minute drive."

"What are we waiting for, then?"

We climbed back in the car. Sebastian had organized for two of the bodyguards to escort us. They looked like they came from the same cookie cutter; both had strong jaws and muscles bulging in places I didn't know there could be muscles. Both wore black tactical pants, black shirts and military-grade cross-draw vests with assorted accessories and all the bells and whistles they required for their guns and knives. One was dark like cocoa and had a head so closely shaven that it shone, while the other had an olive tan and a buzz cut.

The bodyguards sat on either side of me in the backseat, with their broad shoulders squashing me in the middle and their legs spread, keeping me pinned. I pressed against their legs with mine to force them to give me some space. They picked up on my discomfort and eased up on their manly posture. I patted their legs like the good dogs they were and said, "Thanks."

We weaved through the light morning traffic and reached the warehouse Sebastian had mentioned. It was in a rundown part of the city where no one dared venture alone. No streetlights worked. Some buildings were in various stages of decay, while others were empty shells. This warehouse was in great condition; I surmised someone had to live inside it to keep it that way.

I was right. As we reached the side door, it opened, and a man greeted us. There must have been alarms that triggered our arrival; I doubted the man slept on the floor near the door.

The man was slightly taller than me, had sandy

blond/brown hair ruffled from sleep, and despite being relatively short on top, it still hung over his ears and almost in his
eyes; it was in definite need of a trim. He had pretty green
eyes with long black eyelashes that made him appear a little
feminine, but the square jaw and stubble made you think
otherwise. He had a swimmer's physique which was high-
lighted by the fact that he had no shirt on and only wore silk
boxers.

"Sebastian, you should have told me you were coming. I
would have made the proper arrangements." His grin held
mischief.

"Don't sweat it, Lee." Sebastian pushed the door wider and
Lee stepped out of his way, bowing his head slightly as Sebastian walked past. "Lee is part of my leap and lives here to look
after the place."

I remembered the term leap. It's what people called a group
of leopards, so that would make Lee a were-leopard. From Lee's
posture, I could only assume that Sebastian was the leader of
their leap or higher up in the ranks than he was.

We followed Sebastian while Lee closed the door behind us
and came running up to the front to speak with Sebastian. I
couldn't hear what they were saying, but their heads nodded,
and Lee allowed Sebastian to walk in front.

Lee fell back to walk beside me, giving me sideways glances
as if to get a good look. I felt like pushing him away from me,
but I didn't know him, and I didn't feel like pissing anyone off
just yet.

The hallway opened into a large room filled with various
boxes and containers. Other rooms branched off to either side. It
was so spacious that you could easily store a commercial
airplane in there.

"It's this side, Sebastian," Lee said, as he broke away from us and moved to the far right-hand side. Sebastian remained at the head of the group, and we all followed him.

We stopped in front of a row of six containers with various numbers on them.

"When did the consignment come in?" Sebastian asked.

"All six came in about six days ago," Lee said, pointing at the containers.

Hmm—all on the same night I was attacked.

"Which one has the number '369182' on it?" I asked as we walked to the far end of the row.

We stopped short of the second-to-last one, and Lee pointed to one that had rust on the sides and its doors held in place by an old lock—an ancient lock, perhaps something from the 1700s.

There was a noise behind us. It sounded like someone running in sneakers, and they squeaked against the floor with each step. The two bodyguards lifted their guns and aimed at the approaching man, who stopped abruptly and lifted his hands.

"Don't shoot! This is Kai." Sebastian touched the first guard's gun and lowered it to the ground.

Kai was as tall as Lee, but with a lot more muscle. His hair was shaved on the second shortest setting, and he had deep-set brown eyes. His aquiline nose, cheekbones and chiseled jaw reminded me of a Roman soldier. He wore silk boxers and sneakers with no socks.

"Sebastian," — Kai did the same respectful bow, — "I wish you had warned us. I would have dressed appropriately." He grinned with a naughty twinkle in his eye as he glanced at us then back at Sebastian.

"No formalities tonight, Kai. We just need to get inside this container. Do you have the key?"

Kai glimpsed at the container and its lock and shook his

head. "It arrived that way. We don't have the keys for any of them."

"Who brought them here?" I asked.

Lee and Kai both stared at Sebastian, as though asking him for permission to answer my question. He nodded at them.

"One of the young vamps brought them from the shipping company. He said that Léon wants these here and that we are not to touch them—period." Kai answered, but his eyes nervously said something else. Were there other warnings?

I stepped closer to the lock and held it in my hands. It looked as though it was made of strong metal—it wasn't a lock that could be picked or cut through. As I held the lock in my hands, my mind wandered to my pocket. I wasn't sure that it would work, but I pulled the key chain out of my pocket that held the three ancient keys and tried the first. Nothing. The second key made a clicking sound, but I couldn't turn it all the way. The third key clicked and turned all the way, and the lock opened. I stared at the open lock, and my mouth fell open.

Sebastian hovered over me and asked, "Are those the same keys I found in the alley?" His left arm came around me, his hand brushing against my forearm, and took the lock from my hands.

I turned around in the circle of his body. He was too close to me, and I instinctively moved away until my back hit the container. "Yes, you found them in the alley. But I don't know how they are connected?" I swallowed hard, staring up into his piercing eyes.

Maybe the were-animals who had attacked me dropped the keys, and I said as much.

Sebastian thought about that, and his shoulders relaxed. "We will have to speak to Danny, but let's see what's inside first."

It relieved me to be out of Sebastian's penetrating gaze, and grabbed one side of the door while he took the other, and we opened the container at the same time. The gust of air that escaped from the container was rancid, and it blew some strands of my hair as the vacuum created by the container being closed was finally released.

The bodyguards reached for the flashlights on their vests and illuminated the contents within; there was only a sarcophagus resting in the middle of the container on a wide floor made of wood. The boards creaked underfoot as Sebastian and I entered; the flashlights moved as the others followed behind us, but I didn't take my eyes off the coffin. It matched the sarcophagus in the photos. Someone had wanted me to find this, and that same someone must have left the key chain for me to find. But who was helping me, and why couldn't they help Léon themselves? Unless it was all just a coincidence— but I didn't much believe in those.

Sebastian and I gripped the lid of the coffin at the same time, and the others followed suit. Sebastian and I stood across from one another, and Kai and Lee stood beside him while I had the two bodyguards on my side. Ralph remained outside the container. Was he afraid or would he only help when all hell broke loose after we opened the lid?

We started lifting together. It moved easily, and we all coughed as dust rose from the inside. We lifted the lid, and Sebastian, Kai and Lee moved around to our side of the coffin to lay it gently on the floor near the wall of the container.

We went back to the base of the coffin to see what was inside. As in the photos, it contained the mummy wrapped in its black-and-gold linen, and, there, at the cadaver's feet lay three of the most beautiful jewels I had ever seen. I was no expert, but each one appeared flawless, a potent emerald star sparkling against the gloom each time they caught the light from the flashlights.

At first, I was entirely captivated by them, but as I started to regain my senses once more, I stared at Sebastian and wondered whether he would reach for them first or if I should. No one moved.

"What the fuck are those, Sebastian?" Kai asked, protecting his face from the dust particles that danced in the air around our heads.

"Something that can fuck with the master. Do you have a bag for me, Kai?"

"Yeah, sure; let me get it." We could hear Kai's shoes squeak as he ran.

"Aren't you going to destroy them?" I asked.

"That's up to Léon, Blaire. It was his decision for the jewels to be shipped from Egypt, and now that we've found them, I'll take them back to him. We need to find out who did all this; the audacity to hide them in one of Léon's own warehouses, only confirms that the culprit is someone who has access to it all—someone on the inside." Sebastian raised both eyebrows.

Kai's squeaking shoes echoed around us as he ran back with a drawstring bag in his hands, which he handed to Sebastian. Sebastian turned to me, clutching the bag, then he stared at the jewels. Was he afraid that direct contact with the jewels might do something to him because he was a were-leopard?

"Do you want me to pick them up?"

He nodded, handing me the bag, and I carefully reached for the first one. When I touched it tentatively with my finger, there was nothing, just the coolness of the gem against my skin. I picked it up and placed it carefully into the bag, and then I did the same with the other two.

Once all three jewels were safely in the bag, I closed the top and slung it over my shoulders. There was nothing to it; I didn't feel any different. I didn't feel like the jewels were any threat to me. There was nothing dangerous about them.

Sebastian stared at me with wide eyes like something had suddenly struck him.

"What's wrong?" I asked, unmoving.

"I don't know. I sense an uneasiness—or something." As Sebastian said that, the were-leopards raised their heads and sniffed the air.

"What now?" I asked.

"Someone is here—and there are lots of them," Sebastian said.

"How do you even know?"

"We can smell the oil on their guns."

"Shit."

The two bodyguards to my left drew their guns and held them in a ready stance. They started walking out of the container first. It was their job to protect us, and they readied themselves to do so.

Ralph started backing away from the container until the warehouse wall stopped him. He stared at me with wide eyes and mouthed, *"What's going on?"*

I hurried toward him and grabbed his arm. "There are people here, and I don't think they are friendlies."

Kai and Lee joined us, and Lee said, "Follow us."

We did, with Sebastian close behind us.

Glass shattered overhead and rained down upon us. Jagged shards sliced a few scrapes on Ralph's face as I sheltered my head with my hands. Kai and Lee were bleeding, too, but I could see their skin almost instantaneously knit together as they healed. Ralph saw it too, giving me wide eyes. I glanced back at Sebastian, but he showed no emotion. He had his blank face on, the epitome of focus, and I wouldn't have wanted to be in his line of fire. He had his own gun out, ready to shoot at anything that came near us. I didn't notice he carried his own firearm; he must have kept it in a holster at the small of his back.

Kai and Lee led us to a door in the far corner of the warehouse. I didn't see it until we were right upon it. Lee opened it and started ushering us through. We followed Kai while Lee brought up the rear. I heard gunshots behind us, and as we started running, there was an explosion that shook the building. We fell to the ground as the walls vibrated from the aftereffect. When Kai stood up, so did we.

We continued walking at a fast pace until we reached a drain cover in the ground. Kai pointed to it and said, "This is our way out. It's disgusting, but I am sure whoever is out there will have the building surrounded and will shoot at anything that walks out of here."

Kai and Lee lifted the drain cover, and I held my breath. The stench of feces and piss made my eyes water. I lifted my shirt to my nose and mouth, hoping it would help with the smell, but it didn't. I also needed both hands to climb down the ladder into the drain. Shit.

We climbed down into the bowels of the underground, hoping we didn't bump into any unsavory critters while we were trying to run away from the men with guns upstairs. Lee closed the drain in time because he said he heard men running our way and we had to move faster.

We started running in the sewage-infested water, which ruined my shoes and jeans. I felt slime move into my socks as I sloshed in the murky water behind Kai and Sebastian. Ralph was awfully quiet behind me. I thought he was trying not to throw up—as, I guess, we all were.

I thought too soon. Lee was the first to puke. Luckily, he was behind us and I didn't see it, but I heard the retching.

When he finished, he caught up with us, and then it was Ralph who stopped and blew his chunks. I had to walk away from him.

"How much farther?" I asked through the muffled shirt I was now holding in front of my nose and mouth again.

Kai didn't look back. "Not much; there is a clearing just up ahead."

"Thank God," I whispered.

Ralph caught up, wiping his mouth, and I dry-heaved. I kept telling myself I wouldn't throw up… I wouldn't throw up… But I couldn't hold it down, stopped, and I threw up.

Ralph patted me on the back and waited with me until there was nothing left. A shiver ran down my spine, and I wiped my eyes dry with the back of my hand.

"Argh, I don't think I can stand this filth much longer," I groaned.

"I know; me neither," Ralph said, and started pushing me along so we could join the other three.

When we reached them, we stood in front of a large wire mesh that was too thick to cut through.

"I hope you have a plan to get us out of here? Look at that thing—there is no way we can cut through it." I started to complain, but Sebastian lifted his hands and touched the thick mesh. He closed his eyes, and his power rolled off him, around and through us, onto the wire. The effects of his power hit me in waves of heat. It felt like my skin would peel back and burst into flames, but nothing happened to my skin. The thick mesh and the sides that held it in place, however, started to drip onto the floor.

"Jesus," I whispered, rubbing my arms and hugging them close to my body.

Sebastian let go of the mesh, stepped back, lifted his right leg and kicked the mesh from its hinges, and it went flying out into the clearing.

Kai and Lee walked through first. They scanned the surroundings and gave us the 'all clear' signal to follow them.

The drain ended at a clearing where an old building stood, which I suspected had probably been responsible for cleaning water years ago. Now, the building lay in ruins amid lush trees and overgrown shrubs. We all stopped at an open fresh water feature and washed our hands and faces. Those of us who threw up rinsed our mouths.

I marveled at Sebastian as I walked past him. "You don't take shit, do you?"

The corners of his lips reached his cool green eyes, and he looked both handsome and dangerous. "It's good to have me on your side, Blaire."

As we traversed through the clearing together, he lifted his hand and touched the small of my back under the bag I was carrying. There was power at his fingertips, and it flowed through my spine and caused my breath to catch. I glanced over my shoulder, my lips parted, as his power pulsed through my body.

Sebastian's smiling eyes softened, and he bent forward, his hand still on my back and his mouth closer to mine. I was transfixed between his power and his body, and I stood there, waiting in pleasurable anticipation.

His lips brushed mine gently, and then he kissed me. The kiss started softly at first, as if waiting for me to push him away, when I didn't, he kissed harder, and I allowed him to explore the inside of my mouth. He cupped my face in both of his larger hands, and I wrapped my arms around his waist, my hands feeling all that strength under his clothing. This was the second kiss we shared, and it tightened my stomach and other, more intimate parts just as it had the first time, like butterflies trying to escape.

He pulled away. I groaned breathlessly. Sebastian's passionate kiss ignited a fire within me, breathing life into my soul and fanned embers I was yet to discover. Selfishly I wanted more.

When he let go of my face, I opened my eyes. I lost a few I.Q. points because all I could do was stare at him.

He chuckled and gave me a chaste kiss with his addictive soft lips. "I'm glad I have that effect on you."

I couldn't speak; the only thing I could do was nod stupidly at him as a small squeaking sound escaped my lips.

"Come, we need to catch up with the others," he said, proffering a hand.

I focused on the others and they were quite a distance ahead of us. I grabbed Sebastian's hand and we ran to catch up to them.

I glimpsed back toward the opening of the drain, which was void of bad guys. With a tinge of regret, I thought of the two bodyguards who we had last seen back inside the warehouse. With all the shooting going on, it was likely the last time anyone saw them alive.

But I had a future to look forward to, and with Sebastian by my side, I felt as though I could get through anything.

Twenty

When Sebastian and I caught up with the others, I asked, "Where are we going?"

Kai turned to me and said, "We have a safe house over there," — he pointed to a neighborhood where children were playing, — "where we can hide and clean up before moving out again."

The sun was out and hot, and I was sure we all stank something awful. The residents could most likely smell us a mile away. We reached the safe house without being seen by any neighbors or being followed by the bad guys. Lee and Kai checked the perimeter of the house first before we entered. Once we were inside, Lee washed his hands and went into one of the rooms to retrieve a stack of towels and clean clothing for us.

"Sorry, these might be too big for you." Lee handed me some clothes and stacked a towel on top.

"I don't care; I just want to get clean. Thank you."

"Use the shower at the far end. It's the nicest." He winked and headed back to the room for more clothing.

I made sure the shower was on its hottest setting so that I could burn all the crap off my body, and I washed my hair twice until it smelled of nothing but shampoo. I dried myself and dressed in the clean clothes. Lee had been right; they were slightly big. The jeans hung loosely on my hips, and the shirt was baggy, so I tucked it in.

I towel-dried my hair with the same towel I had used on my body. I left my dirty clothes in the room, but I removed all the contents from the pockets and put them in my new jeans.

When I finished, Ralph went in after me. Lee had used the first shower already and was already making coffee in the kitchen while Sebastian was cleaning up.

Kai chuckled when he saw me. "Jesus, those clothes are way too big for you, luv. Lee, you sure there isn't anything smaller?"

Lee turned to look at me and shrugged. "Sorry, that's all we have—we rarely have women with us, and when we do, they aren't so small."

"Don't worry about it, guys; this is perfect. I'm just glad to be clean." I smiled appreciatively. "What must I do with my dirty clothing? And are there extra shoes?" I stood barefoot, the cool tiles a comfort to my aching feet after wearing the wet socks and shoes.

"Yeah, we might have, although they're probably steel-tip boots."

"That's okay; add socks, and I'm happy."

Kai went into the room where they kept the extra clothing and came out with a pair of black steel-tip boots and black socks. "Here, luv—these should fit you."

"Thanks, guys. And the coffee smells good." My smile reached my eyes. My body ached, but we were safe. After the hot shower and clean clothes, I felt better.

"Almost done," Lee said, starting to take food out of the fridge.

I pulled the socks on, followed by the shoes; they were new and stiff, but they were my size.

The first bathroom door opened, and Sebastian came out with steam trailing him like a halo. He had a towel wrapped low around his waist, and I fought hard not to stare at his inguinal crease and chest. He gazed at me as he crossed the hallway and went into the other room.

I felt hot under the large shirt.

Kai went into the bathroom next.

Lee approached with a steaming cup of coffee; grateful he took my mind off my salacious thoughts. I thanked him and enjoyed a sip. I relaxed in the seat and sat back, put my feet—boots—up on the couch, and hugged my knees with my left arm. I leaned my head against the couch, only lifting it for sips of coffee.

With my eyes closed, I listened to the sounds of the house. Lee was in the kitchen; I heard him retrieve a pan from a cupboard and placed it on the stove, the tearing of a packet and the opening of an egg box. The first bathroom shower was turned on. I heard Ralph switching his shower off, and then little else from him as he was probably getting dressed. There was no sound from Sebastian. I heard the birds outside as they flew around the house. I heard whistling and the faint laughter from children playing outside. I felt a smile forming on my face as I exhaled.

"You look very peaceful."

The mug tilted and almost spilled its contents on the couch and my lap. I sat up.

Sebastian loomed over me while he slowly dried his chest. He wore low cut jeans, but was naked from the waist up. I watched him dry himself in front of me, and my hand started to burn—I had spilled coffee over my hand, but only felt it now.

"Jeez, you need a bell, Sebastian. I didn't hear you walk across the room." It's a wooden floor; I should have heard him—at least one footstep—but I didn't.

"I'm a black leopard, Blaire; no one can hear me," he smirked.

"No shit. But hey, after what we just went through, at least warn me next time," I grinned.

He gave a throaty chuckle, threw the towel onto the couch and went into the kitchen. Lee gave him a mug of coffee, and returned to sit beside me on the couch.

"Now what do we do?" I asked while staring into his luscious green eyes, so close to me. There were a few drops of water on his chest, and I wanted to lick them off him. By being so close to me, Sebastian was intolerably distracting, and so I glanced at Lee, and I felt better.

"We eat," he said. "While we do that, we can see what the fuck happened at the warehouse."

"How?" I said, turning my attention back to Sebastian.

"Cameras. We can tap into the feed from here."

"Ah."

"Where are the jewels?" he asked me.

"In the room with my dirty clothing. Should I go get them?"

He nodded. I set the mug on the table and went to the room. The door was open, and when I entered, Ralph was pulling pants up over his naked ass. I swore, held my hand in front of my eyes and turned around.

"I'm done, Blaire. You can turn around."

"Fuck. Sorry, Ralph, I thought you were dressed already." I grabbed the bag from the floor and exited as fast as I could.

Still feeling hot in the face, I sat down on the couch and took my mug. I offered Sebastian the bag, but he didn't take it.

"Just keep them with you, always. I don't want to have to hold them or have them too close to me."

I placed them at my feet on the floor, and we drank our coffee in silence.

The smell from the kitchen tickled my nose, and we all circled the counter like vultures. Lee must have been a chef in a previous life because the food was presented like a pro, and when we started eating, it tasted like nothing I'd ever eaten before. The scrambled eggs were light and fluffy; the bacon was crispy, but not burnt; the biscuits were soft, airy and melted in my mouth.

"Lee, this food is delicious! Are you a chef?"

"I was—before the attack." The flicker in his eyes showed hurt and despair.

There were laws against were-animals working with food, children, any kind of medical equipment or offering any medical care. If that was your profession and you turned, unfortunately, you lost your job. Employers couldn't discriminate against other jobs though; such as boring, mundane desk jobs—so long as you could prove you were in control of your inner animal you kept your employment. The downside was you could only prove that after a two-year probation period assessed by animals of your own kind.

I didn't know what to say to Lee, so I thought it best not to say anything. From the expression on his face, I doubted he wanted to speak about it—some men just didn't want to get deep-and-meaningful, anyway.

"I was in the military when I was bitten," Kai said, breaking the silence. "They wanted me to stay on, but I didn't like how they pushed were-animals, especially the predators. They used them on the frontline like they were expendable, just because they could heal and were a little harder to kill. It was barbaric. And they tested on some of them, too. So, I left without permission and came here. Sebastian took me in, and I joined his leap. That's when Léon offered me a job." His smile held sadness I could only imagine. He carried on eating with no emotion, like it had been somebody else's story he told.

I lost my appetite, pushed food around the plate and finished a second cup of coffee.

I'd heard some of Sebastian's story already. Him being the leader of his leap certainly matched his image. He seemed to fill the room with swirls of dominance, and power surrounded him, along with a splash of danger. At first glance, Sebastian seemed like the cute boy next door—gentle and kind—but something else lurked beneath the surface; a spine-chilling darkness that consumed him if pushed too close to the edge.

Ralph had eaten less than I had and was pushing his food around his plate, too. "Ralph, are you all right?" I asked.

Even though I didn't really remember, I'd supposedly known Ralph for years, and the new me had never known him to be this solemn during the last few days we had spent together. There was something wrong; he was distant, tired and not all together there.

"I don't know what's wrong," he replied glumly. "I started feeling down the moment you opened that coffin."

When we had opened the sarcophagus, Ralph had been the only person not in the container with us. I reached out to touch his arm, but he flinched like my hand was on fire, even though I hadn't actually touched him. I took my hand back and stared at the large man who hunched over his plate.

"You were the only one who wasn't near the coffin when we opened it. Maybe something happened to you because you weren't near it?" I was spitballing. "Maybe if you touch the jewels, or stand near them or something, you might feel better? I don't know. You want to try?"

"Maybe," he shrugged.

I got up from my chair, picked up the bag and placed it next to him on the table. Sebastian, Lee and Kai got up from the table and stood on the other side of the room near to the front door. I didn't know what to expect, but nothing happened. Ralph sat, still staring down at his plate. He rubbed his arm again.

"Is that where the witch touched you?"

He glanced at his arm. "Yes, it tingles." He rubbed it again.

"Seraphine touched Ralph when she was busy removing the curse from me. Can we trust her?" I asked Sebastian.

"She has helped us in the past, but one can't be too careful when it comes to witches."

Whatever was happening to Ralph, it was the last thing we needed.

"Do you feel ill, or are you just... quiet?" I asked tenderly.

"I don't know how to describe it," he said, touching his arm again. The skin beneath his fingers was visibly pink. "It feels sensitive."

"Maybe you should stop rubbing it; it's turning pink," I grinned. I wanted to ask if he was in shock, but he was an assassin—I doubted anything shocked him anymore. Even so, his was strange behavior for an assassin.

"Do you have Seraphine's number?" I said, but Sebastian wasn't in the room anymore. I glanced down the passage to see if he'd moved to one of the other rooms but I couldn't be sure.

I opened the bag with the jewels, picked one up and handed it to Ralph. I shrugged. "Maybe hold one, I don't know. We aren't the ones with powers to lose, so maybe they affect us differently. Not sure if the jewels do anything to the leopards, but they're standing out of the way."

Ralph took the jewel from me and held it in both his hands. I couldn't describe it, but one moment the spot where Seraphine had touched him was pink, and the next his skin was light brown again. It could only be courtesy of the jewel.

"I think it did something, Ralph," I said, pointing to his arm. "It's not pink anymore." Even Ralph's cheeks had color again.

I picked up another jewel and held it in my hands. I could feel the stone's power calling to me, and picked up the final jewel and held the two I had close to the one Ralph was holding. The moment the three jewels touched, an incandescent light emitted from them and shone on the ceiling. I flinched and stood back, separating the three jewels; as soon as that happened, the light disappeared.

Sebastian came running into the kitchen. "What the hell was that?" he said, rubbing his arms.

Kai and Lee entered behind Sebastian, they too were rubbing their arms as though they were cold.

The hairs on my arms stood on end, but I felt nothing else. "When all three jewels touched, they created a light. Let us show you." We repeated the process. The moment all three jewels touched, a light shone out of the middle where they connected and reflected onto the ceiling. We held our arms still so the light would stay. Ralph lifted his free hand and let the light brush against his fingers.

"Does that hurt?"

"No, it's just a normal light. Well, normal for me," Ralph said.

"Any of you want to try your hand through the light?" I asked the were-leopards.

Kai pushed Lee forward. "You go first."

"Pussy," Lee said, stomping forward. When he reached us, he lifted one of his hands and waved it through the light. Nothing happened. Then he stopped moving; the light hit the palm of his hand. Still, nothing happened. "What's it supposed to do, anyway?"

"Control vampires," I said, almost nonchalantly.

"How?" Kai asked, moving closer to us and running his hand through the light. "It tickles and burns a little if you keep your hand there," he said, continually moving his hand through the light like he was trying to chop it up.

"Sebastian, can you still feel your power? I don't know what you call it, but can you channel your power?"

He closed his eyes. "Can you feel that?" he asked, opening them again.

"What?"

"Shit."

"Is it affecting you?"

"Yes! You sure you can't feel anything?"

"No."

I waited expectantly to experience once again the very power that had earlier trickled along my skin, the power that had so easily turned that wire mesh into molten slag, but now I felt nothing—not even a breeze. I pulled the two jewels away from the third and asked, "Try now."

As I spoke, his power flowed over me like heat running over the sides of my body and around my waist. It raised the hairs all over, and my body started to curve backwards. "Yup, I can feel that. You can stop it now." I smiled at him, and then I frowned.

His smile reached his eyes, and he knew what he had just done. "I guess that means the jewels work on were-animals, as well."

"I guess so." I rolled my eyes.

"Pack the jewels securely," Sebastian said. "We can't afford for any of them to be chipped or cracked. Miles is on his way to fetch us. He should be here within the next hour or two."

"I'm lying down until he gets here," I said while yawning.

"We will tap into the warehouse camera feed," Sebastian said. "Maybe we can see who attacked us."

Twenty-One

S omeone touched my shoulder. I opened my eyes and saw Ralph. He sat on the edge of the bed, still holding my shoulder.

"Miles is here; we need to go. They will drop us off at my car, and then we'll meet them at their house, place, whatever it's called, to hand the jewels over to Léon. Apparently, none of them want to handle the precious artifacts."

"Oh, okay." I begrudgingly moved my legs to the side of the bed and stood up to follow him.

All the guys were waiting for us in the living room.

We piled into Miles's Jeep with Sebastian riding shotgun, me in the middle with Ralph on my right and Kai on my left, and Lee in the back on one of those chairs that folded against the side.

"Sebastian, could you see who stormed the warehouse?" I asked as Miles drove us through the late morning traffic.

"No. They were all wearing black, and their faces were covered. We couldn't see a thing."

"So, you don't know who did it?"

"No," he said, not sounding entirely happy about it.

The traffic was light, and after twenty minutes, we parked behind Ralph's car. As I reached the passenger side, I turned in time to see Sebastian walk toward me. With his loose limbs and strong muscles, he walked like a large cat. He stopped close enough to touch me.

"Follow us and park where we park. I don't want Léon's guests knowing you're in the building." His tone made my arms pebble and the expression he wore left me on edge.

"I don't understand." I frowned. "It can't be because we are assassins. What's the real reason, Sebastian?"

He opened his mouth and then closed it again, glancing back at the occupants of the Jeep before turning back to me and whispering, "They are not the most sociable of vampires, Blaire. They will chew you up and spit you out."

"Why? They don't know me?"

"They love toying with humans, and if they found out you're an assassin, they'll certainly sink their fangs into you. They are worse than Ian and Esther."

I shuddered at the thought. Enough said.

"Do the other vampires know what Léon did—about the first mark on me? If I remember correctly, they have some kind of metaphysical link to one another, or to one directly from their line."

Sebastian's shoulders slumped slightly, as though he was holding onto something that had hurt for so long it was straining them. He exhaled, the sound suggesting he could finally breathe properly again.

"You seem to know a lot about vampires."

"Honestly, I surprise myself. Almost every minute, I keep remembering little tidbits of information. It's mainly generic details; nothing personal at all, really. It's like my brain is still alive, but there's just no memory of who I am."

"You are right, Blaire." He sighed audibly. "That's the reason why the other vampires are here. They sensed something had happened, but they don't know what it was. If they saw you, in the flesh, their link to Léon would allow them to see exactly what happened, hence he doesn't want you brought anywhere near them."

Léon had promised he wanted nothing from me in exchange for giving me the first mark. That he only did it to save my life.

"Will he be punished for what he's done?"

"It's possible."

"Shit, I didn't know that."

"I hate vampire politics."

"What I can't figure out is why they care so much as to whether he has a human servant or not? I thought vampires had free choice in things like that. Léon is a master vampire; surely he can choose who he wants?"

"Typically, that is the case; master vampires can take on any human servant they choose. But this is the council, and all vampires still have to answer to them."

"Why do they care who his human servant is?"

Sebastian hesitated. Finally, he said, "Léon is over eight hundred years of age. He has been around the world a few times and in all this time, he has never had a human servant—not once. A master vampire can take on a human servant, and if the servant dies, the master, if strong enough, may survive and take on another. But," — he tried to find the right words, — "Léon is stubborn. There was a human, once, who would have been the perfect servant for him, but he didn't want her. Eventually she became a vampire, and now she is extremely powerful herself.

She sits on the council, and it is she who is here demanding to know what happened."

"Is she the jealous type?"

"Very."

A horn sounded, and Miles started yelling out of the window for Sebastian to hurry.

"In a minute," Sebastian yelled, holding up his hand to tell Miles to be patient.

"What's her name?"

"Who?"

"This jealous vampire."

"Galina. She's quite something, Blaire. I hate being in the same room as her." He shuddered. The memory of how Galina made him feel seemed to take Sebastian aback, and he started to shiver, even though the air was warm and there wasn't a wind. Whatever she did to him seemed to linger just beneath the surface of his composure, along with his inner animal.

He pulled himself out of his daydream and held his arms. The shivering stopped, and he tried to smile but failed. It was unusual for Sebastian. He actually looked scared.

"She cannot know who you are," he warned.

"I definitely don't want to meet her, thanks. What is she going to do to Léon?"

"Fuck knows. I don't want to be around when it happens though." He paused to run his fingers through his hair. "But Léon needs me, and he's expecting me to be there. Galina won't start anything until I arrive, so we have to go now."

Miles honked the horn again, but Sebastian ignored him. His sparkling green eyes paled and showed a little more white than before. Even though I had only known him for a few days, he was usually much more confident than this. He pulled himself together, shook his body and put on a smile that almost reached his eyes. The tension in his jaw was gone as he exhaled, like he was able to release himself from that bad memory.

"It will be okay," he said reassuringly. I suspected he was trying to convince himself more than me. "Just stay out of sight." He touched my elbow and squeezed.

"Are you sure we should even go there? It doesn't sound like we should," Ralph said as I climbed into the car. As I got comfortable in the passenger seat, Ralph was racking the slide of a pistol he had reached for under the seat.

"I know; I don't like it either. Do you have a spare gun for me?"

Ralph's smile broadened, and his eyes sparkled with a hint of mischief. "Look in the glove compartment. At the top, there is a latch. Press on it and see."

I did as he said and found that there was a Glock 19 Gen4 inside the secret compartment. As I took it out, it fit into my hand perfectly. How I knew it was a Glock 19 Gen4, I didn't know, but I liked the feel of it in my hand.

"Cool. Hopefully, I have the guts to shoot it. Does it have silver bullets?" Yet another piece of information that swam into my mind, for which I had no explanation.

"We can't kill them with silver, but it does enough damage to slow them down." He pulled away from the curb and followed Miles's car.

"If Galina comes after me, I want to protect myself long enough to either get away or come up with another plan."

"I hope it won't come to that, but if you need a knife, there's one under the carpet beneath your feet."

I lifted the carpet to find, as promised, beneath it was a tactical Benchmade 810 Contego Pocketknife. As I lifted it and turned the stainless-steel handle over in my hands, I noticed it even had a butterfly engraved upon it—the symbol of our organization. The knife flicked open to reveal an extremely sharp blade that could easily stab through a vampire's cold, thick skin.

"Cool, I like the Benchmade 810 Contego Pocketknife. It's not too heavy and fits easily in my hand. Thanks, Ralph."

"You know the make?"

"It's strange. I'm remembering bits and pieces of things, but not all. At least it's something, I guess." I shrugged.

We were still behind the other car and driving at the speed limit, the smoothness of the road and the surrounding trees almost hypnotic and tranquil. I tucked the gun into my pants at the small of my back and pocketed the knife. I rested my head on the seat and closed my eyes for a moment.

The water was warm and thick, like a blanket comforting me from the cold. I opened my eyes, and the water was maroon. The tree that always seemed to pop up in my dreams was on the shore, but it was different now— it was hollow and ashen.

The motion of the crimson waves pushed me to shore, and I walked up the rich, silky sand that shimmered beneath my feet, its fire-like color shifting between red, yellow and maroon. I knelt and touched the tree where its bark met the sand, and the earth fell away. Below was only darkness, and as I looked into the chasm to see what else was there, I fell inside. I floated and fell all at once, like the air was nothing, exactly how I imagined Alice felt when she visited Wonderland. When my stomach didn't flip with the sudden motion, I reached out to the sides, and as I did, I stopped and looked down.

My feet came to rest on a cold floor. The bedroom was inside a cave, with a bed in its center and platinum silk bedding that looked smooth and inviting. To the right of the bed stood a dressing table with a high-backed chair in front of it, and on its left, was a wardrobe. Near the only door was an antique mirror with an engraved mahogany frame that stood apart from the rest of the furniture.

As I turned to reach for the door, a woman appeared before me. She was slightly taller than I, but her posture seemed to magnify her height until it began to feel as though she was looming over me. Her startling, vivid green eyes revealed the evil within her—a power so great I felt it pulsing through the air. Her hair, the color of the whitest of snow, fell like a curtain around her shoulders and ended near her hips. Her black eyebrows offered a shocking contrast to her pale skin and the white of her hair, and beneath them, her green eyes seemed to illuminate in the dark cave. Her thin lips curved upward in a shallow smile, revealing her sharp fangs.

I stepped away, but she grabbed my arms.

"So, you are the one who has caught his eye," she hissed. "You are not much to look at, so there has to be some other reason as to why he chose you." Her deep, piercing eyes raked over my body, and it felt like tiny insects biting my skin. The sensation was almost scalding.

"You must be Galina?" I said through gritted teeth.

"Oh, so he has spoken of me?" The insect bites stopped, but her grasp still felt hot against my skin.

"Not quite, but I've heard a few things about you." I felt beads of sweat run down the side of my face.

She dug her fingernails into my skin, and they were sharp and painful. I felt liquid trickle down my arms. Her face was close to mine, her breath warm and smelling of blood.

"You smell of old blood," I said, lifting my face upward and away from her, but still kept eye contact.

She cackled as I tried to get free from her grasp, but she held on tighter.

"What is so special about you? I do not see it." She shook me as she spoke, almost as though she wanted to emphasize the fact that there was nothing special about me.

The old Blaire might have killed her, once. The new Blaire was a little scared.

"There is nothing special about me, Galina. Nothing," I yelled.

She sniffed the air. "You tell the truth, but you are still unsure of many things, human. Your mind is clouded. There is something blocking you from truly seeing." She tapped my forehead with a long fingernail. "I can set it free, if you like. I can release the lock on your mind."

I shook my head too quickly, a '*gah*' sound escaped my lips, and the nausea started to build. I wanted nothing from her. I didn't want to find out what she could offer, and I certainly didn't want to know what she wanted in return.

I wanted out of this dream. Out of her grasp. OUT!

She let go of my left arm, and her right hand brushed hair out of my face. With her fingertips, she touched my cheek, and with that soft touch, her back bowed and her green eyes rolled into her head until I only saw white.

With all the strength I had, I pushed her away from me with both hands. She let go of my other arm and fell, but before she hit the floor, she disappeared in a cloud of dust.

I was left gasping in the car seat.

Ralph jumped in his seat. He turned the steering wheel left, then right as he corrected the car. Other cars flashed us from ahead and others honked their horns from behind or next to us.

I caught my breath while Ralph kept us from crashing.

"Blaire! What the hell was that? Are you okay?"

It was already dark outside, and relieved Ralph couldn't see the tears on my face.

"It was her, Ralph. Galina invaded my dream. I can still feel her on my skin." I started to shake. I brought my knees up to my chest and wrapped my arms around them.

"Damn it. We are here, Blaire. Maybe we shouldn't follow them inside. What do you want to do?" Ralph slowed the car and turned right, stopping behind the Jeep.

"Stop right here. I don't want to go in. She knows who I am, Ralph. She knows, and she isn't happy."

Ralph made a U-turn, ramped up the pavement, and stopped.

Sebastian must have seen what we did because Miles stopped the Jeep before they entered the garage and Sebastian walked toward us. He approached the car and knocked on my window.

"What happened?" he said as I opened the window.

I was shaking, rocking in the seat.

"I saw her, Sebastian. I fell asleep, and she invaded my fucking dream. She fucking touched me! I can still feel her like she was inside me." I shuddered, tears streaming down my face.

"Shit." Sebastian sighed like he was tired, defeated. "There's no way you can come inside now. No fucking way." He looked over the roof of the car. "Shit, they're here," he said, under his breath.

I turned to see what he was looking at, and Ian, the vampire who had tried to bite me—the vampire who was supposed to be locked in his coffin—was stalking toward us. He was swaying his hips wearing a malicious smile across his face.

"Start the engine, Ralph. Let's get out of here." I hit Ralph's hand so he would start the car.

Something hit the bonnet; Esther. She dented the car so badly it wouldn't start; Ralph kept turning the key, but all we got was the clicking sound of a dead battery.

Roland was suddenly beside Sebastian, and hit him so hard

that Sebastian flew across the road. Then, Roland bent down to rest his arms on the window, his head close to mine. "We've been waiting patiently for you, little one."

"What are you doing, Roland?"

"Galina wants to meet you."

"Did you let them out?" I asked, motioningtoward Ian and Esther.

Roland was supposed to be on our side—on Léon's side—but the glimmer of evil that swept across his face told me otherwise. He would not help us, and he would take great pleasure inflicting any pain Galina asked him to do.

"What did you do to Léon?"

"Nothing… yet." His sadistic smile was back.

I was angry, hurt and scared, but anger seemed to be the most I felt. The vampires had us surrounded, but something in my training told me I needed to see how this played out. I reached for the drawstring bag containing the jewels and secured it over my shoulder. I wished the stones didn't need to be held in order for their power to be unleashed, as they would have instantly diminished the threat the vampires currently posed, but I also knew that now was not the right time. Whatever they had planned, we needed all of them to be together.

With that in mind, however, I couldn't wait to test the jewels out on these assholes.

I unlocked the door, twisted my body toward it, unbuckled my seat belt, and pushed as hard as I could when I opened the door. It was not the best thing to do because the only thing that happened was Roland fell on the floor by my feet and laughed. Well, at least I was entertaining.

Sebastian started running back to us, but he couldn't get past Esther and Ian. Esther was holding him from the front while Ian had his arms pinned behind him from the back. I couldn't see what Esther was doing to him, but she was touching him in places I didn't think he wanted her to touch. He struggled between the two vampires, but eventually, Ian appeared strong enough to restrain Sebastian on his own.

"What is so special about you, Blaire?" Esther yelled. "Why does Sebastian and Léon want to keep you safe?"

I didn't know, either. I shrugged, but she didn't see me. Roland was off the ground and gripping my right arm, and started pulling me toward them.

"She must be good in bed or something, cause I sure as shit don't see it either," Roland said, pushing me into the back of Esther, who turned around to catch me before I bumped into her.

"I like the taste of her, though." Esther licked her lips and hissed.

"What is with you fangers? Can't you just leave me alone?"

"I love it when humans get angry; it spices up their blood," Ian said from behind Sebastian and let him go. Then he started walking around the were-animal to stand beside Esther.

"Come, Galina is waiting for us," Roland said, grabbing my arm again.

Twenty-Two

W e left Ralph's car outside on the pavement and entered the warehouse through the garage. Darkness spilled around us when the large metal door hit the ground. I saw spots before me as my eyes adjusted to the change, and I flinched when someone grabbed my shoulder and walked beside me. I was calmed by the smell of waves of the ocean, citrus, fresh leaves and wet grass. It was Sebastian.

"Just stay near me," he whispered near the shell of my ear.

I wrapped my arm around his waist so that I could walk where he walked. I was sure those leopard eyes saw perfectly and would stop me from walking into things. After a few steps, a dim light came on, and I saw we were inside a large garage containing twenty cars. Some were old and dusty, while others were new and clean. One was a limo, while another was a sports car—there was a car for every occasion.

We followed Ian through a door that led us down a narrow hallway which branched off in three different directions. We continued along the middle one.

After descending a small flight of stairs, we entered a large banquet hall with gas torches adorning the walls—they provided enough light to see everybody in the room. The walls of the banquet hall were high and dark, so dark they appeared black. The soft light from the torches barely challenged the shadows, offering the room a sense of deepest night.

As we approached, there were people in the room I didn't recognize.

Léon had his back to us, but I knew it was him by the broad shoulders and stance; the confidence a man of his esteem had gained. He was wearing a long black coat over an outfit I couldn't see.

Galina had her hand on his shoulder and spoke close to his ear. Everything about the situation screamed 'old lovers', but since I couldn't see his face, I wasn't sure whether he was enjoying her conversation or not.

As we entered the hall, everyone turned to stare at us.

Were-animals, dressed in black, lined the walls, standing ready to protect Léon. And just off to one side, I saw Miles lurking in the shadows.

The air was mildly suffocating from all the power radiating within the confines of the room—the power produced by each of the vampires staring at us, each hinting at their strength.

Heat danced along my skin like hot water droplets from a shower. The burn spread across my skin like molten lava flowing down a hill. I shivered and rubbed my arms, hoping it would stop.

Léon spun around, his eyes flitted between Roland, Ian, and Esther. "Who released these two?" He pointed at Ian and Esther.

"It was me," Roland said, closing the gap between Léon and himself.

"Why?"

"I thought we might need the help. My humble apologies if I was wrong."

"You continue to defy me, Roland. This is becoming a common occurrence," Léon said, a hint of warning suppressed behind his words. He leered at Ian and Esther, evidently unhappy. "They can stay for the night, but then they must go back."

Ian and Esther stood closer to each other and held hands. They stiffened when Léon said they were to return to their coffins. Good.

There was a tall man beside Léon. His straight hair was more salt than pepper and was kept neatly off his face. From where I stood, his skin was pale and smooth, and he had small pouty lips, a thin nose and high cheekbones. His eyes looked like they could either be blue or dark gray. He wore a black high-collar mandarin suit with silver loops sewn on, the patterns moved when he walked.

The man glided toward Sebastian but kept staring at me. They embraced in a half-hug while the man spoke in French. I didn't understand what was said, but it sounded pleasant; there was no shouting or high-pitched sounds, and they both smiled like long-lost friends. With them standing so close and their faces together, they shared similar facial features.

Léon glided over to the two men, and the three of them shared a group hug. Again, with all three standing so close to one another, it was those high cheekbones and jawlines that made them all strikingly similar.

I stared as all three turned to face me. I realized the older man had blue eyes, a shade lighter than Léon's dark ocean blue.

Léon spoke first. "This is Salvador, our father."

Salvador glided over to me with an outstretched hand. He had long delicate fingers and wrapped both hands around my hand, kissing the air next to each of my cheeks. He smiled, still holding onto my hand.

"So, this is the Blaire everyone has been running around to meet." Salvador glanced over his shoulder at Galina. I didn't know what look he had on his face, but Galina's mouth pulled askew and her green eyes narrowed.

She lifted her hands into the air as if chasing a fly away from her face. "What would you expect? This is most sudden, is it not?" Her glare moved from Salvador to Sebastian.

Sebastian couldn't keep eye contact with her and stared at his feet, and then at me.

I didn't need a mirror to know what was on my face. The lines between my eyes deepened, and I gave him one of my blank stares and shrugged.

"She doesn't know it was you?" Galina asked, and then she laughed, a high-pitched cackle that would burst your eardrums if it was any louder. I had the urge to cover my ears, but then the laughter stopped, just as abruptly as it started.

Looks were shared between Galina, Léon, and Sebastian, but no-one spoke. Salvador glanced at each of them and grimaced, and then his mouth blossomed into a smile. He was enjoying whatever was going on.

"Will someone please tell me what is going on?"

I folded my arms across my chest.

Léon approached me with his stony face hiding whatever he was thinking. When he was close enough, he placed his hands on the side of my arms.

"We had to lie to you, Blaire. It was not I who marked you— but Sebastian." He considered his brother and tilted his head toward me as if telling him to comfort me.

I didn't want to be held by either of them. I thought about

what Léon had said and didn't understand it. "Wait, what? Sebastian is a were-animal. Can you mark humans?"

"I'm a hybrid, Blaire," Sebastian said gently. "I'm part vampire, part were-leopard. I'm the best of both worlds."

"Why not tell me from the beginning?" I didn't understand why they had lied. It wouldn't have mattered either way. They saved me—both of them.

Sebastian stared at me and stopped to stand beside his brother.

My arms were still crossed. I didn't want anyone touching me. If they did, I might just go for the gun and start shooting.

"We had to lie to you because we weren't sure what you would do if you found out it was me," Sebastian said, trying to explain. "As you know, people are still unsure of were-animals, and there is more supporting literature on vampires than my kind. If you wanted to research it, you would have found that what Léon told you was plausible. We didn't know who you were. And I couldn't tell you what I truly was. Not yet.

"My secret is just that, and you can appreciate the risk to me if I shared my secret with a human I just met. But you need to know, Léon did first try to mark you, but it didn't work, and you were dying. When I tried, the mark took, and you started to heal. We suspect it was because I was a different were-animal to the one that attacked you and I had the additional vampire powers to heal you."

Roland laughed, and I flinched. He closed the gap of our little circle, still laughing. "Sebastian is a *half-breed*; a lesser vampire and a lesser were-animal. He is just lesser. And Léon is too selfish to help anyone—his sole focus is strengthening his power base. He doesn't care for anyone but himself."

"I tire of your constant ramblings, Roland!" Léon responded. "Do I not give you enough power to manage the club?"

"Ah, but that is the problem, old friend. It is your club; it is your power you lend me."

The conversation was moving too fast and in different directions. I was trying to keep up with who had marked me, and now there was this tension between Roland and Léon. Roland was powerful, but I doubted he was more so than Léon. The air seemed to thicken with a sour stench, and I raised my hand to my mouth.

"You need to control your rot, dear friend. Even the human can smell it." Léon turned to Roland, and the two vampires leered at each other.

I was missing something important. I didn't understand how Roland's power was rot, when in the club, it had felt like desire and pleasure.

Sebastian stepped away from them, pulling me with him.

"Sebastian is more powerful than you'll ever be, Roland. The only reason he must hide it is because of what he is. Because of who he is, as my brother."

Roland yelled in French, and they didn't sound like happy words.

"Your temper sets you apart from me, my old friend. If you were truly a master vampire, you could have left my court and established one of your own. But it's what I have that makes you stay. It's the power I share with you at the club that keeps you there. Do you believe if I were gone, you could continue offering pleasure to so many all at once?" Leon's face grew grave as realization dawned upon him. "It was you who tempted fate with your greed."

Roland fell silent and nodded slowly with a wrathful grimace.

Léon pressed on, like he was poking a stick at a snake,

waiting for it to strike so he could kill it. "What makes you so miserable, old friend? I thought you were happy."

"It is true. I wanted you gone, I wanted you dead."

Power rolled off Léon upon hearing Roland admit it was he who wanted him dead, and it took my breath away. Roland fell to his knees, clutching at his throat as if he was struggling for air. Somehow, Léon was able to choke Roland without even touching him; the effect on Roland was surprisingly great, given that he was such a powerful vampire himself, rendering him powerless.

"No, Léon, it's not worth it," Sebastian said, edging closer and almost grabbing hold of Léon's arm. "Think of the consequences! You can't have the council against you."

With one hand, Léon caressed the air in front of him and Roland could 'breathe' again.

I could breathe.

"I should kill you, Roland, but I need to hand you over to the council. They will see to your appropriate punishment."

Roland's eyes flitted from Léon then to Miles. As he tried to recover his composure, a smirk began to form on Roland's lips. "Perhaps I'm not the only one deserving of punishment, Léon. After all, I didn't act alone. I had Miles assist me."

Everybody turned to stare at Miles.

"Miles?" The pang of betrayal was evident in Léon's voice. Léon turned to his security, the man he entrusted to keep him safe. His eyes widened, but fury slipped into his expression. "What have you done, Miles?"

Miles paled, and he looked like the proverbial deer in headlights. He avoided Léon's gaze. "It is true. At first, I helped Roland, but I later changed my mind. I stopped the assassin." Miles's eyes flickered in my direction. He paused for a second, then said, "I'm sorry we attacked you, Blaire—my brother

Danny and I. It was regretful, but it was my duty. When I saw you following Léon that evening, I knew you would kill him, and I couldn't allow you to do it."

To Léon, he said, "Please forgive me, master. When I learned of Roland's true nature, I knew I'd made a grave mistake. He said he would make me his second-in-command, but I knew a were-animal could never be second to him. He was only using me like he does everyone else."

Roland made a gruff sound.

"Was it a crisis of conscience?" asked Léon.

Miles nodded. "Yes, master." He walked over to Léon, bowed, then went onto one knee and asked for Léon's hand.

Léon offered him his hand and Miles kissed it.

"As much as I want to make an example out of you," Léon said through gritted teeth. Then he glanced up at Sebastian. "I need to hand you and your brother over to your respective animal groups to maintain the peace treaties I have with them." Léon stared down at Miles who kneeled before him. "That said, it doesn't mean I have to hand you to them unharmed."

Léon made a hand gesture as if to strike Miles, but the blow did not connect. Instead, his bladed palms sliced through the air, and Miles and Roland both cried out in pain. Each had received a deep lash across their backs, and blood pooled from their wounds.

All this had happened to me because Roland had a bug up his ass to take over from Léon, for which I was furious. Roland had Miles arrange an assassin—me—to take Léon out, but when Miles changed his mind, probably because he realized that Roland was the bigger asshole, he attacked me instead, to stop me. That attack had nearly killed me.

"Why the hell didn't you just tell me—our company— that

you wanted to cancel the contract? You didn't have to leave me for dead, Miles," I yelled. My chest and neck hot.

I balled my hands into fists and remembered the gun at my back. I pushed myself away from Sebastian and grabbed the gun from under my shirt. I flicked off the safety, aimed and fired. I didn't think about my actions; I just did it. It was muscle memory at its best. The first shot hit him in the gut, and the second one struck him in the thigh. I moved the gun from side to side, aiming at anyone who came closer. Everyone stayed away, including the guards.

"You messed me up, Miles. I think it's only fair I do the same to you."

Miles crumpled to the floor, blood pooling beneath him.

"Get Mel!" Sebastian yelled to a nearby guard. The were-animal nearest the exit turned and started running.

"Is it loaded with silver bullets?" Sebastian asked.

"Yes," I said in a low voice; my tone held no emotion. I knew this was my true voice, the one that came from a dark place deep inside me. That was me—the real me—the assassin that went to a place that was iniquitous and quiet.

I was still holding the gun, ready to shoot anyone who came near me.

"You two," — Sebastian pointed to two of the guards, — "carry Miles to Mel." They did as Sebastian ordered and picked him up, carrying him away.

"Thank you, my dear," Roland said, his voice cutting through the tension. "Hearing how Miles deceived me, I would have killed him myself, but you've done all the hard work for me," he grinned.

He was pissing me off. All this had happened because of him and I fired twice into his neck.

He clutched his wounds with both hands and made gargling

sounds as blood poured from his neck. I wasn't worried. I knew he would heal. He was a vampire. I could rip his throat out, and he would still heal. What I needed to do was take his heart out and chop off his head.

Roland fell to his knees, with one hand at his throat and the other flat on the floor in front of him so he wouldn't fall over. I heard wheezing and bubbling sounds from him and it made me ecstatic knowing he was struggling.

Léon laughed, the sound surprisingly pleasant and therefore disturbing in the circumstances. It rolled in the air and surrounded us like a warm hug. His laughter usually felt as though it caressed the soul, and so to hear it as Roland was gushing blood upon the stone floor was chilling. He motioned for two guards. "Place him in a coffin and lock it with a cross. He can stay there until the council are ready for him."

My arm was burning from holding the gun up, but I kept it aimed at everyone. I wasn't sure whether I would be the next one to be dragged away and locked up, and so I would protect myself.

"Was it you, Roland?" Sebastian asked as they carried Roland away. "Were you the one who stole the mummy and the jewels?"

Through the bubbly gargles, he laughed, and the guards who were dragging him stopped. I struggled to hear him speak, but I understood most of what he said.

"Yes, but I couldn't touch the jewels." He laughed, and more bloody bubbles leaked from the holes in his neck. "No vampire can hold the jewels. They are meant for humans to use against us." His laughter spilled through the large hall, and he coughed some more. He lifted his hands up for us to see the burn marks on the palms of his hands. It wasn't the bottle of holy water he caught as he had first claimed. It was obvious he tried to harness the power of the jewels, and they ended up scarring him instead.

Léon motioned for the guards to continue escorting Roland out. He combed his fingers through his hair to remove the few loose strands from his face. His blue eyes were now pale—icy—as opposed to their usual inkiness, and reminded me of husky's eyes. As the color seemed to change with his mood, I wondered whether this light color reflected his happiness?

Léon walked to me, placed a hand on the gun and lowered it.

"Nobody will harm you, Blaire. I promise. Please lower the gun before you hurt someone else. This is not something I ever thought a vampire would say—but I think there has been enough bloodshed for one evening." His eyes sparkled with humor.

I did as he asked, but I kept the gun in my hand, just in case.

From behind us came a loud, "No!" and Galina floated toward me.

My reaction was painfully slow because all I saw was a blurred vision of her as she knocked me to the ground. Her shrill cry piercing my ears. She straddled my waist and pinned my hands to the floor above my head. The gun had been knocked out of my hand as her body collided with mine, and the drawstring bag had flown across the floor with the gun. The force of the assault stunned me for a moment as I tried to focus on the angry vampire baring her fangs beneath wild green eyes. Her white hair covered both of us, and I smelt peppermint—she must have taken my criticism to heart when I said she had smelled of old blood in my dream.

"Get off me!" I struggled to get out of her arms, but she was much stronger. She could throw a small car over her shoulder without breaking a sweat.

She gripped my wrists tighter, and pain shot through my

outstretched arms down to my shoulder blades. I wanted to cry out, but I didn't want to give her the satisfaction of my discomfort.

I stopped writhing beneath her and leered at her—her pale skin, her black eyebrows, her piercing green eyes, and her pursed thin lips.

"You took him away from me!" she yelled, spit landing on my face.

"Who? What are you talking about?" I said between shallow breaths. Although she was thin, she sat heavily on my ribs, and it felt like a rock was crushing me. I had to stay focused.

"Sebastian! I'm talking about Sebastian," she shouted. "He was mine. All mine! Then you came along and took him away!"

It was Sebastian all along, and not Léon, who had been the subject of Galina's jealousy.

Her green eyes bled to something darker, a mixture of seaweed and maroon. Her eyes were growing in her anger, and she shoved that anger into me. It tore through me, causing my skin to feel as though it was burning and my blood felt as though it was on fire, eating its way through both muscle and flesh.

"I didn't take anyone away from you!" I yelled back at her.

"Get off her, Galina," Léon said.

I heard footsteps approach us from my left, dress shoes clicking on the marble floor. I heard more footsteps come closer from my right, and I hoped they would remove her soon; my breath was shallow, and my lungs were burning.

As my lungs filled with her power, I felt my life draining away. I took my last shallow breath and stared into those dark green eyes, wanting to tell her she could have him. It was so not worth it. I wouldn't fight over a man, no matter who it was. But

I couldn't speak. I couldn't do anything. I simply watched as her death grip rendered me immobile.

As someone pried her fingers away from my wrists, someone else picked her up and carried her, kicking and screaming. As the two men removed her from me, Ralph kneeled beside me. He had the drawstring bag in his hands, and opened it.

With Galina no longer weighing me down, my lungs filled with air. My body was slowly coming back to life, one limb at a time.

Ralph helped me to sit up and gave me one jewel while he held the others. We pressed the jewels together until their bright light shone upon the roof in a blaze of vermillion and the air cleared.

All power evaporated, and the vampires fell to the floor. They didn't scream; they didn't make a sound. They weren't in any pain that I could tell. They were just... quiet.

Sebastian was only half a vampire, but it still affected him just as much as the others. He was lying on the floor with Galina next to him and Léon on the other side. All three turned wide eyes on me.

Salvador had remained where he was, only now he was sitting on the floor with his legs crossed. A smile reached his eyes, as though our actions had impressed him. He tilted his head in my direction, in recognition. He was an odd vampire; we had removed their powers, yet Salvador seemed delighted.

Ian and Esther had crumpled to the floor and crawled into a fetal position. They definitely weren't as powerful as the others, as the effect of the jewels seemed to affect them the most.

Ralph and I kept the jewels pressed together. We kept that light shining toward the ceiling and allowed to reflect around the hall.

"P-l-e-a-s-e!" Sebastian said through gritted teeth. "Please, stop." He started to hunch over, as though he was holding his stomach in place.

When we first pressed the jewels together at Léon's warehouse, it had been for a mere few seconds, and as soon as Sebastian had said he couldn't use any of his powers, we stopped. But now, we kept the jewels pressed together, and the longer we did this, the harder it was on the vampires. I felt the smile on my face reach my eyes as Ralph and I shared a knowing look. His smile matched mine.

"Cool," Ralph said. "What are we going to do now?"

"I don't know." We couldn't keep our hands like this forever. Also, because their power had never been documented, I didn't know if there was a threshold for how long the jewels could be pressed together. Nobody knew whether the jewels power would cause the vampires discomfort, pain and then death, or they would only remain powerless. Everything was experimental.

"Let me kill her," Galina yelled through clenched teeth. She lifted her head from the floor and started a slow crawl toward me. If she had been angry with me before, now she seemed livid.

"Stay away from me, Galina, or I will chop your fucking head off!" I pulled the pocketknife from my pocket, flicked it open and pointed it at her. "Don't fucking move. I have had enough of your shit for one day."

Galina stopped mid-crawl, then rested her forehead on the floor on top of her hands. "Please stop!" she cried, and, this time, I heard a quiver of pain in those words.

"Give me your word you will leave me alone, Galina."

"Yes! Yes, you have my word! Now please stop. Please— please stop it!" Her wounded words echoed throughout the hall, leaving me feeling selfishly happy.

"Please, Blaire, no one will hurt you," Léon said. "The tie that binds you to my brother is a double-edged sword; if they hurt you, they hurt him." He made a slow turn to look at Sebastian, and his eyes showed sorrow, not just in pain from what was happening to them now, but from years filled with a hurt that they both shared.

I was an assassin, but I couldn't do it. The person I was now wouldn't torture them. I wanted to take their hurt away. I wanted them to find happiness. It made little sense to me, but that's how I felt. I was tired, I was sore, and I had had enough.

I turned to Ralph, and he knew the look in my eyes. He withdrew the two jewels he held against mine just enough for the light to instantly dissolve.

Nobody rushed to grab us because nobody wanted us to press the jewels together again. They knew we would if they tried to hurt us.

The vampires stayed where they had fallen.

Salvador rose from the floor in one swift motion, as though he had been pulled up by strings. I lifted the jewel I held so he could see I would use it again if he came any closer.

He held up his hands. "I just want to talk, if I may?" He stepped closer, both hands still raised in the air.

I lowered the jewel back into my lap, but Ralph kept the two in his hands relatively close to mine, just in case.

Salvador straightened his dark suit by brushing down over his body, and, to me, it looked like a nervous gesture. "I think we all need to take a step back and breathe—metaphorically speaking for us vampires." He grinned. "We need to appreciate the severity of those jewels and to respect the new owners of them. I don't know about you, Galina, but I don't want to piss off this woman any more than you already have. Agreed?"

"Yes," Galina nodded furiously. "Yes, I won't anger her, especially if she can wield those jewels to such extremes."

"Good. So, do we have an arrangement?" Salvador studied me, the silver patterns on his suit snaking over and around his body.

I gazed into his light blue eyes, then looked at his nose because I wasn't sure if he would use his vampiric wiles on me. Vampires had the ability to mess with you and make you do all sorts of crazy things you would never otherwise do—sober, at least.

He smiled. I think he understood why I wasn't looking him in the eyes.

"Yes, we all leave each other alone so we can all live tomorrow." I stood and focused on his nose—just in case.

"Léon, are we eventually going to dine in this fine banquet hall, or do I need to source my own food for tonight?"

"No, Father, there is food—even for the humans," Léon said, standing up from the floor. He managed one leg at a time and then stretched his spine backwards until there was a crackling sound. He held his hand out for Sebastian, who hesitated at first, but took it and stood up.

"Are we talking 'willing' food?" I asked as I met Léon's gaze.

He nodded. "There are still plenty who will even pay us for taking their blood, but I don't need their money. We will however reward them with our pleasurable desires, Blaire." A mischievous smile stretched across his face like a lazy cat out in the sun. "My chefs will bring out your food soon. I believe it's roast beef and vegetables."

I wasn't up to eating, but as I thought about it, I realized that I'd only eaten once today.

Léon and Sebastian left Galina where she had fallen, and they joined Salvador at the large dining table.

I stayed a little back with Ralph and waited for all the vampires to reach the table before we joined them. Ian and Esther went to their master and sat on his side. Galina sat next to Salvador on the far right. Jean-René and Charlotte entered the hall, just in time for dinner, and sat with the rest of the vampires.

Ralph and I were the only humans who were technically invited to sit at the table; Elena and the other were-animals were still littered across the room as guards.

I picked up the bag of jewels and swung it onto my shoulder, picked up the gun, and placed it once more at the small of my back, tucked into my jeans. I had to shift it around until I was comfortable with it being there.

All the vampires occupied one side of the table, so Ralph and I sat on the other. I faced Sebastian while Ralph sat on my left and faced Léon.

A row of humans entered the hall, all led by a male guard I'd never seen before. There was one person for each of the vampires; they stood behind their respective vampire's chair and waited.

Two guards entered with trolleys of food in silver dishes and set the dishes in front of myself and Ralph. The largest dish contained roast beef and chicken while two smaller dishes were filled with roast potatoes and an assortment of vegetables. From the other trolley, a guard removed a bowl of rice and a brown sauce and set them upon the table. The food smelled downright delicious now that it was right in front of my nose. My mouth began to water, and a slurpy sound escaped my lips as I breathed in the aroma.

"Please begin, Blaire, Ralph." Léon gestured for us to start. He looked at the vampires and gave a curt nod, and they all stood together to embrace their meals standing behind them.

Sebastian, however, stayed in his seat. Since he was half-vampire and half-were-leopard, I wondered which meal he would dine on this evening.

He watched me with his hawk-like eyes. Léon touched his shoulder, and he stared up at his brother as Léon said something to him in French.

Sebastian shook his head glanced back to me, and said, "No, brother. Tonight, I will eat real food." He stood up from his seat and came to my side of the table, plated some food and sat beside me.

Ralph and I followed soon after him. We ate, and it was every bit as scrumptious as it smelled. Another guard poured red wine, which we drank, and we ate while the vampires sank their teeth into their willing human offerings. Loud gasps slipped from human lips as the vampires rolled their minds to help them enjoy the feeding as much as they were. The dark-haired woman in Léon's arms opened her mouth wide as her eyes rolled back into her head. She looked positively orgasmic as Léon held her, one arm around her waist and the other resting on the side of her face to give him extra room to bite down.

As I watched Léon, I wondered what his bite would feel like, and as I thought it, my eyes drifted to Sebastian and I began to wonder the same.

Epilogue

R alph and I were well fed—and, thankfully, still alive —by the time we left Léon's residence. We offered our goodbyes to Léon, Sebastian and their guests and returned to Ralph's car, where we agreed that we were in no hurry whatsoever to return.

Ralph bunked with me for a few nights in the basement at my house, where we kept ourselves safely locked away to recover from our ordeal.

Nightmares plagued my slumber, but Ralph was there to comfort me through all my screams and tears, holding me late at night or early mornings, while I fought not to go back to sleep.

During the day, we would leave the basement for fresh air and sunshine. Ralph took me to all the places he thought I would recognize and he hoped might bring back pieces of my mind. Some places were vaguely familiar, while others I just couldn't place, but he didn't stop trying.

I asked Ralph why Ulysses Assassins didn't have an office anymore, and he said it was for security reasons and that our phone number had to keep changing. I suspected he was trying to hint that it was because my daughter had almost been kidnapped, but I didn't feel like talking about it yet, so he didn't bring it up again.

He showed me how we ran the business. It was mostly via the Internet, which was a smart move, according to him. We were sitting ducks if we stayed in the office. There were crazy nuts who didn't approve of our business and had tried to harm us before. He explained our contracts came from private clients via Slayerbody, or from the police. He used the term 'officially/unofficially' and confirmed that contracts sanctioned by the police were reserved only for those cases where they couldn't catch the monster themselves.

Fortunately for me, Ralph knew the bank where my safe deposit box was kept. Desperate to access my daughter's information, I tried the remaining two keys on the hieroglyphics key chain to see whether they would open it, but none of the keys worked. That meant I was still in possession of two keys that would open locks somewhere, but I didn't know what they would open, where these locks were or who had given me the keys. It was just another mystery that, right now, I couldn't solve.

One afternoon, Ralph and I were going through the photos we had had developed, and when we put the blurry photos together and arranged them in a certain way, they formed an obscure, blown-up picture of my face. It creeped us out—me more than Ralph, admittedly—as we realized that someone had taken the pictures of me at close proximity. Yet another mystery I didn't have an answer to.

The two witches, Désiré and Seraphine, came back to me like they said they would.

Désiré asked for the identity of the witch responsible for the curse on me, but I claimed I didn't know. I told her the man who had attacked me had confessed and begged for forgiveness, and as a result, we were cured. She didn't need to know the whole truth; after all, I might need a favor from Seraphine one day.

Désiré had consulted one of her covens' oldest books and located two paragraphs that explained the 'gift' she thought I had. It wasn't common at all, and as she had predicted, it enabled the human recipient to absorb power, syphon it and then use it as and when required. She said that the fact that my aura glowed pure white was a very good sign, and she promised to help me. We could meet up once a month so she could help train me in my new ability and all things witchery.

Seraphine also shared with me one of her covens' books. It started out explaining what my ability was, and although the description was similar to Désiré's definition, there was one difference—the witches who uncovered humans with this particular power were to be sacrificed. No wonder there weren't that many of us around. Most, if not all, had been killed.

I had red flags screaming in my head when I heard this.

This was possibly the reason why I kept my ability a secret, but I didn't know how to hide it now, as I had once done. I wondered whether the brightness of my aura gave me away or if there was something I was missing.

I asked Seraphine why the other witches killed humans who had this ability. "Once a human syphons power from a witch, that power can be used against all other witches," she answered. "It is like taking a curse, reversing it and lashing out at all the others, but the difficulty comes when the human doesn't know how to control their power."

I asked her if she would help me to understand exactly what I was capable of and to teach me to harness my ability. She agreed on one condition; she would teach me only for as long as my aura stayed white. If I began to learn of my power and my aura changed, it would mean I was changing into something else. A white aura was something sacred, Seraphine had said, as pure as I was going to get, and it would enable me to stay connected to the spiritual world. In her coven, a pure white aura was a sign of good intention. In order not to be slaughtered by Seraphine's coven, I would ensure my aura stayed white.

At least now I had two witches who would teach me all their spells and incantations so that I could use them to defend myself. I had no interest in using them to hurt others, and I made a promise to myself to only use these powers when necessary. We scheduled my training to start next week.

After a week of silence from Marcus, we started to worry about him, so Ralph began an intense search and got a ping off his cellphone. We found him in an alley; he was in a worse condition than before, but we brought him home to my basement to recuperate. We were able to nurse him back to health, and when he could talk, he did.

Marcus explained how he met a fellow were-lion, a scientist named Melinda Cromwell. She had been trying to cure them both of their inner animal. When she thought he had overdosed on her latest batch of 'cure', she dumped him in the alley to die, like trash. He cried, even though he had only known her for a short time. He said he loved her and wanted to be cured. He reasoned that if she wanted to be cured, then so did he. I wanted to tell him that if she loved him, she wouldn't have dumped his ass, and that nothing could cure him of his animal, but I didn't say any of that. I think he understood what had happened to him, and he had paid the price. He lost two fingers from his left hand to gangrene because he wasn't able to shift into his animal form and heal himself in time.

Every other day, I went to the shooting range and practiced

shooting with different guns, or I went to the gym, where I would spar with some of the fighters. My strength was improving, and my scars were healing better than they should in such a short time frame. I guess I had the vampire/were-animal mark to thank for this little gift. I still wondered about the second mark though and whether it would change me, but I didn't want to know for sure. I didn't know how much it would change me, and that was what scared me the most.

I'd experienced enough change in the last month to last me a lifetime. And I planned to take things one step at a time.

Sebastian called often, but I answered none of those calls.

I now understood why I had such a strong attraction toward him, but I had no way of knowing if it was the mark that made him attractive to me or if it was him as a person—or both. So, for now, I was avoiding him.

Ralph said I was being stupid and I should meet up with him; that I only lived once, and I was still young, yada, yada, yada…

I would see.

I first needed to fit the pieces of my own puzzle together before I could even think about seeing anyone, no matter how much I liked them.

From Me

Dear Reader

I write in as many genres as I love reading in. There are so many stories swarming inside my head that I could never just choose one.

Horrors are my guilty pleasures. I love writing short stories filled with dark humor and the occult with a twist ending.

Urban fantasy and Paranormal Romance are where I love to spend my time and I have so many books planned that I don't have enough time (*but I'll get there*).

And lastly, my **thrillers**. Who doesn't love sitting on the edge of their seat while reading about what goes on inside the antagonists mind. Well, I love writing about them.

You can view all my books on my website. They come in ebook format as well as paperback, and most are in hard cover.

I've politely asked my family not to read any of my books as I'm afraid they might look at me differently. But you are more than welcome to read my pretties—they are waiting to be devoured by you (*so what are you waiting for? Go on, have a look. I'm waiting…*).

Come find me at the usual hangouts, say *hi*, and tell me about yourself.

Until the next book, stay safe and keep reading.

Thanks for Reading

If you enjoyed this book, please consider **leaving a review** at the site where you purchased it from? A one or two line would be fantastic. Each review helps authors like me reach new readers. *Thank you!*

Also by

Short Story Collections

What's for Dinner?

The Hunter

The Package (Make Them Pay Anthology)

Book of the Dead

Horror Features Series

Creature Features

Monster Features

Dana Mulder Thriller Series

Nightcrawler

Deadly Pattern

Devil Mountain

Chasing Evil

Dana Mulder Omnibus

Stand-alone Thriller

Lady Killer

Blaire Thorne Urban Fantasy Series

Ulysses Exposed

Voodoo Priest

Butterflies & Hurricanes

Salvation

Blaire Thorne Omnibus

Underworld Legacy

Shifter Days, Vampire Nights, & Demons in between Series

Dark Tarot

Wolf Retreat

Lady Hawk and her Mountain Man

The Fixer

Twisted

Night Hunter

Kai

Hidden Shifter

Wolf

Printed in the USA
CPSIA information can be obtained
at www.ICGtesting.com
LVHW092326170524
780601LV00004B/359